BenGee Bucks Publishing Presents

RUN & GUN

A Novel By

Jamal A. Benjamin

This novel is a work of fiction. All names, characters, places and incidents are products of the author's imagination. Any resemblance to actual events or persons, living or dead, is purely coincidental.

Copyright © 2013 BenGee Bucks Publishing

Acknowledgements

Special thanks goes out to the people who provided the motivation I needed to finish this book. My interest in creative writing was sparked at an early age. Marilyn and Ricky, both of you had an incredible role in nurturing my aspirations. My seeds of motivation were also planted by extraordinary individuals who have inspired me with their own feats. David, Shawndella, Rob, Darryl, Cindy, Kurt, Barion, Roble' and Hadiyah, Thank you for your words of encouragement and most importantly your admirable accomplishments.

The love I have for Virginia, Tracie, Janale, Brianna and Judah has no boundaries. This is why I am dedicating this book to all of you. Your unconditional love lifted me over every episode of writers block and procrastination. Thank you for becoming the embodiment of true blessings.

JAMAL A. BENJAMIN

Chapter 1

It was a scorching autumn day in New York City. Even TV weathermen had trouble explaining why it was so unseasonably hot. But the heat definitely made it good basketball weather. The sun baked the blacktop on b-ball courts throughout the Big Apple. Scores of spectators could be seen at any one of the playgrounds—they were all meccas for premiere showcases of street ball talent—but the courts on West 4th Street in Greenwich Village were special. It seemed like the world was watching the players there. Students from the nearby New York University, traveling tourists, and lunch break browsers all began to take notice of the kid who never missed a shot. Walking down a dark alley, most of the faces in the crowd would probably do everything they could to keep their eyes off the teen with cornrows and tattooed arms. There were parts of his exterior that made some spectators initially wonder how many felonies he had racked up, but his caramel complexion complimented by his baby face and skinny frame, made most think Barkley Capleton wasn't all bad. The "can't miss" kid was also able to douse the rush to racially profile him with the 100-watt smile he flashed each time he pulled up for a jumper.

Swish! Another shot made, and he could hear the whispers from strangers as he jogged back down the court.

"That kid's goin' pro."

"Who does he play for?"

"That kid is the truth."

Barkley chuckled to himself as he got back on defense.

"Next basket wins," a man in the crowd said.

"I'm tired of robbing folks, so do me a favor and don't try that bullshit ass crossover," Barkley said to another player. The trash talking had reached a fevered pitch with both sides going out of bounds with disrespectful insults. But it was Barkley who was backing up his words. "Call the cops. Damn, I told you not to try that shit," he taunted as he stripped the ball away from a player on the opposing team. "Now I got three strikes, but only difference is you get the death penalty!" he shouted.

Dribbling the ball between his legs like his fingertips had magnets made by Spaulding, Barkley shook left, then right, and when his defender slipped and fell on his backside, the kid closed the show. "Let me put these niggas to sleep. Goodnight."

Swish! Barkley turned to the crowd of spectators and took a bow. Applause erupted as Barkley left the court. Well-wishers and fellow players came up to him as if he had just won the NBA finals.

"Great game kid."

"What college do you go to?"

"Can we take a picture with you? We love basketball in China."

However, the baller with the boyish looks walked past all of them without even a nod or the smile he repeatedly flashed on the court. His game was over. The escape from the harsh realities of his world had come to an end, and for Barkley, making the return trip to a stressful home life was nothing to smile about. He made a swift exit

3

from the court and dashed down the steps toward the subway to catch the train.

"Next stop Utica Avenue," the A train conductor announced. Barkley sighed and put on his hooded sweatshirt. The train pulled into the Utica Avenue station; the doors opened and Barkley exited the train with his head hung down then began to walk at breakneck pace. He counted down each corner he passed hoping none of the Bloods crossed his path on the way home.

Three more. Two more. One more, Barkley thought.

He reached his block without incident, but began to slow down his pace as he approached his home. Nearing the front door, he heard the yelling and crying from outside. As he pulled out his keys, the front door swung open.

"Wait, wait . . . don't go!" Mother Benson yelled. A middle-aged thuggish looking man with a resemblance to Old Dirty Bastard exited the house shouting expletives at the top of his lungs.

"Fuck you! I don't need this. I don't need no little girl parading around me wearing some little tight shit, begging me to touch her and then yelling rape when I don't. Fuck this."

And out the door he went. He was boyfriend number four within the last five months. Mother Benson had a penchant for choosing pedophiles, jobless low-lives, and parolees. She was the head of the foster home and a hell-raiser for all four of the foster children under her roof. This is where Barkley called home for the past fourteen years, and he did his best to avoid crossing paths with Mother Benson. In his seventeen years of life, Barkley had very little happiness and none of it stemmed from that home. He was three years old when he became the first foster child Mother Benson took in.

His childhood inside Mother Benson's foster home was a horrific experience. Tears spilled from Barkley's eyes each time there was a minor or major mishap in the home. There was the time he didn't make his bed on the day of a social worker's visit. Mother Benson laughed as she jokingly admonished Barkley for the small infraction, but that staged reaction only delayed the severe repercussions he later suffered. Mother Benson unleashed her wicked wrath only moments after they were left alone. She handcuffed him to the radiator. Unfortunately, that was only the beginning. He received lashes with an extension cord as she scolded him for what she called "making her look bad."

From the ages of four to seven, Barkley was the prime target of Mother Benson's reign of terror. She only took him out of her crosshairs when two new children arrived. Both were sweet young girls, but that had no bearing on how they were treated. Barkley actually thought their gender made their experience much worse. Mother Benson always had men coming in and out of the house. The kids wondered how someone so mean could manage to like sex so much. Most of her lovers were weird in their own way. There were the ones who had wives who always thought they were being watched. The pastors from church who thought they could mask their true intentions with private Bible study sessions. Then there were the monsters. Some of the men were verbally abusive, while others committed more heinous acts. Sabrina was eleven years old when she moved in. Nicole arrived months later at the age of twelve. Both were free-spirited, pretty girls who fell victim to one of Mother Benson's pedophile boyfriends. He molested both for over a year. Barkley recalled the fear he felt one night when he attempted to get into bed with Nicole. He would always head to her room after awakening from nightmares. Her room was no longer a sanctuary after he witnessed an act scarier than any nightmare he ever had.

He froze when his eyes locked with Nicole's as Mother Benson's boyfriend, Kyle, pumped his penis into her. He watched as his foster sister's innocence was being ripped from her. Barkley eventually mustered up the courage to move, but running to tell Mother Benson didn't do him any good. She was stuck in a drunken haze and didn't even acknowledge him when he tried to nudge her out of her intoxicated state. Nicole was never the same after that. It was only two months later when she decided to take her own life. Hanging herself in the bathroom was a better alternative to the life she was experiencing. Social workers and Mother Benson brushed it off as an unfortunate result of bullying caused by her promiscuous behavior. Her schoolmates were merciless after learning she let three boys have their way with her. Barkley knew the truth, but felt helpless to do anything. When the same boyfriend began making moves on Sabrina, he could only turn his head. Sabrina was touched, but luckily she was not raped. Mother Benson walked in on her and Kyle taking a shower. She immediately kicked him out but did not call the police. A phone call to the cops would have immediately cancelled her foster care meal ticket. Sabrina's mother eventually won back her parental rights and came for her. More kids came in and out of the home. And with each new kid, Mother Benson laid down the law.

Having extensive knowledge of the rules and regulations, Barkley was pretty much left alone. He was able to avoid Mother Benson's war path by going outside to play with the other neighborhood kids. When he began to take those trips outdoors, it was at that time he fell in love with the sport of basketball. Every day from sun up to sun down, he was on the court honing his skills. He soon began to generate some buzz on the local playgrounds. Barkley's skill level increased at a meteoric pace. He often played with the adults, dishing out servings of embarrassment to older players at the age of thirteen years old. The same could not be said for his schoolwork. The New York City Public School system was not the appropriate setting for Barkley. He was promoted in grade school without ever really knowing much. This all caught up with him in high school. Failing test scores and incomplete homework assignments kept him from being successful in most of his classes. More importantly, it kept him off the school's basketball team. Unable to join the team because of poor grades, Barkley shifted his basketball focus to pick-up games at the local community center. This is where he met Officer Shamus Harrison.

The NYPD rookie immediately took a liking to Barkley, taking the teen under his wing as if he was his younger brother. Barkley also welcomed the friendship. He most enjoyed talking with Harrison about old movies and attempting to convince him to watch *Martin*. He often told Harrison he was missing out on a much better sitcom experience compared to watching *Seinfeld*. Each time they met up, Harrison would try to steer Barkley in the right direction. The interactions were beginning to spark positive motivation within the teen, when he was forced to cut down on his visits to the community center. Because he was the oldest, Barkley was tapped to be the caretaker of the new foster kids Mother Benson took in.

First came Charity, who arrived when she was thirteen. Her story read like the tales associated with most abandoned children in the 'hood—she was the product of a neglectful mother and a crackhead father. Next were Chase and Kim. Kim arrived three months prior to her brother's arrival. They were fifteen-year-old fraternal twins that should have been kept together when their mother went to prison for interstate drug trafficking, but mishandled paperwork split up the siblings. Chase landed in a foster home full of boys, where only the strong survived. He left the house alive, but was scarred with a permanent limp caused by the two housemates who broke his leg in three places. Some may have thought Kim got the better end of the stick following the separation, but she experienced her own house of horrors with a brief stint inside the foster home of a heroin addict before she was transferred to Mother Benson's. Since Barkley was Mother Benson's first child, he learned early on that staying out of her way was the best method to avoid the madness. To the dismay of Mother Benson's new crop of foster kids, it took each of them a couple of years before they eventually learned how to avoid her abusive ways. Barkley had adapted, but there were times staying out of trouble was impossible, especially when trouble came looking for him. Once Barkley made inside following the exit of Mother Benson latest boy toy, it wasn't long before she interrupted his self-imposed isolation from the rest of the house.

"Barkley! Barkley!" yelled Mother Benson.

Now that he was older, Barkley often ignored Mother Benson. He finally understood he was one of four meal tickets she had, and her big ass loved money and eating too much to get rid of him. However, this time was different. She sent Chase to get him.

"That Professor Klump lookin' bitch wants you, and don't ask me for what. Just come the fuck downstairs so she can shut the fuck up. I'm missing *Project Runway* over this bullshit," Chase said.

As Barkley made his way down the stairs, he wondered what she could possibly have to tell him. He had just recently started asking about his mother's whereabouts. The first thing that came to mind was maybe she had information for him. Barkley lost contact with his mother two years prior. The last time he saw her was inside a prison visitors meeting room. She said she would come for him once she got out on parole. Barkley's mother said a lot of things, but never followed through on any of her promises. Going M.I.A was part of the process. She would disappear, resurface, and disappear again. Most of the times her disappearing acts were drug induced or facilitated by the state's correctional officials. Heroin was his mother's drug of choice. She would often claim to be clean, but the tracks on her arms told a different story.

"Get down here boy!" shouted Mother Benson.

"I'm right here," Barkley replied.

"With you turning eighteen in a couple of months the state has notified me that your well is about to run dry. If I'm not getting money from the state for your ass, you have to do one of two things: get out or fork over some rent."

"You kicking me out?" he asked.

"No, I'm giving you the option of getting kicked out or continuing to reside under my roof. My rates are pretty reasonable."

Barkley was disgusted and made sure his facial expression mirrored his feelings. "You know I don't have any money to pay you and I still have school."

"School? Your dumb ass is a student now? Nigga please. You been in the eleventh grade for how long now? This is grown-up time and besides I'm not going to lose an opportunity to bring another one of you bastards in here if I have the chance. I'm just giving you first dibs before I apply for another foster child. I do have a heart," said Mother Benson sarcastically.

Unfortunately for Barkley, Mother Benson's heart was black to the core and pumped venom throughout her robust body. She was being honest about losing the money. The state would no longer pay her for housing Barkley, but child services was not going throw him out like trash either. Once Barkley turned eighteen, he would be eligible for a stipend and his own apartment unless he wanted to stay with Mother Benson. Without a hint of regret, she neglected to inform him of the government funds awaiting him because that was money she couldn't get her hands on.

"Fine, you fat ass ho! I'm outta here. I've got time. I'll find my mother and go live with her. I don't give a fuck where she's staying. Anywhere is better than this fucking place," Barkley said.

"Boy, your mama ain't coming for you and she damn sure ain't anywhere around these parts or any other place. That bitch died last December in the prison yard. I guess she got tired of eating some big bitch's snatch and tried to fight back. Wrong move on her part," Mother Benson chuckled.

A few seconds of silence passed before Barkley lunged for Mother Benson and grabbed her neck.

"I could fucking kill you right now! You took everything I've ever had. And you couldn't even give me that chance to say goodbye?"

Kim, Chase, and Charity heard the commotion coming from the kitchen. They could all tell something violent was going on, and that Mother Benson was catching the bad end of it. They briefly looked in the direction of the tussling sounds and then turned their attention back to the elimination round on *Project Runway* without moving an inch. The choke hold compressed the air in Mother Benson's throat by the second. Catching a homicide charge wouldn't better Barkley's situation, so he released her from his clutches and walked back upstairs with tears streaming from his eyes.

"You got two months. Two months, you hear me?" shouted Mother Benson.

Chapter 2

Monday mornings were always the roughest for Barkley to get out of bed. He couldn't remember the last Monday he didn't just lie in his bed and just stare out of the window in deep thought. Barkley would begin by immersing himself in fantasies. Announcing the college he planned to attend was one fantasy he often conjured up. Each time it was a different school, but the setting was always the same. The press conference to hear his decision would be attended by every network and newspaper in the country. The television camera lights would nearly blind him as he sat down at the table set up for him. His acceptance speech began with insults.

"I wanna send a big fuck you to all the Bloods and Crips that would chase me home. I can say that because you bitches don't go nowhere and I highly doubt you'll come to kick my ass at the University of North Carolina, which is where I've decided to play college ball. Any questions?"

That morning the Tar Heels was his program of choice, but he fantasized about every big college basketball program in the country. He would then lie there thinking about how he would survive the day. If it wasn't the teachers on his case about his assignments, it was local gang bangers testing him. Avoiding major dust ups with the local riffraff had become easier over time, but today was different. As he made his way outside he could see Justice and his fellow Bloods brethren on the corner. Taking the scenic route to school would take Barkley an extra twenty minutes to get to school, but avoiding a beat down during the early morning hours was his first priority. It proved to be the safest path over the last couple of weeks. He felt he had to travel that way since he had words with Justice's cousin, Juvie, on the basketball court three weeks prior. To most basketball fans, taking it hard to the rim is an example of good competitive basketball, however, in the twisted mind of Juvie, it was a total embarrassment to get dunked on. This was grounds for payback. Juvie had every intention of giving Barkley a buck fifty across his face with the box cutter his friend slid him while the park spectators were in a frenzy. Lucky for Barkley, his best friend, Born, saw what was about to go down and blocked his friend from receiving 150 stitches and a nasty scar. A stare from Born and quick wave of his finger was enough for Juvie to cancel the carving session. Born was Barkley's savior on many occasions.

Both of them grew up on the same block, and when dealing with Mother Benson got to be too much, Barkley sought solace at Born's home, where he lived with his grandmother. Born wasn't a gangbanger, but he had the respect of the neighborhood goons because of his connection to one of the biggest drug dealers in Brooklyn. In the Crown Heights section of Brooklyn, the criminals and low-lives stayed clear of police and anyone carrying a package for Monarch Bolton. Working for Monarch wasn't a get out of jail card, but it did grant a pass in almost any situation that didn't involve bloodshed and catching a body.

With only a block and a half left from the front door of his school, Barkley felt footsteps behind him. As he turned around, he quickly learned that Monday morning was going to be a rough one. He caught a sharp blow to his jaw. The beat down commenced after he stumbled into nearby bushes and was pounced on by four of Juvie's boys before he could gain his footing.

"Stand that bitch up," Juvie demanded.

"It was just a game man. It was just a game. Chill," Barkley said.

"Well, this shit ain't a game right here. You tried to embarrass me in front of my niggas during a friendly game of basketball. Don't you know that I've shot niggas for less?"

"I'm sorry man. What the fuck would you have wanted me to do? I was just playing."

"You was playing? What could you have done? For starters a fucking lay-up would have worked. A jump hook you long, lanky motherfucker. But no, what do you do? You dunk on me and scream as if your ass is auditioning for *SportsCenter*. This ain't *NBA Live* and you ain't about to disrespect me and get away with it."

"Wait, man. Wait, man. I'm sorry."

"Hell yeah, your ass is sorry. And your punishment is gonna cost you more than two points. Yo, son, pass me that pipe out of my bag. Let's see if you dunk on anybody else after this."

"It ain't that serious man! This shit is crazy," Barkley said, still trying to reason with Juvie.

Ignoring him, Juvie took the pipe from his friend and got into a batter's stance. He swung, but missed.

"Hold this nigga's leg! I'm trying to get this shit done before homeroom. One of y'all bend down and a grab his legs!" Juvie yelled.

The gangbanging crew grabbed Barkley, ready to give him a beat down, but they had a monkey wrench thrown into their plans. A glass bottle shattering into pieces on the concrete near their feet forced them to divert their attention away from turning Barkley into a cripple. Juvie turned around to see where the diversion came from and who was bold enough to launch it. Born fearlessly stepped forward to take full responsibility.

"We all know how this is gonna end. Let my man go, and we can just call this a huge misunderstanding," Born said confidently.

Frustrated, Juvie yelled, "This got nothing to do with you, Born!"

Born responded with a back-hand slap. "Have some fucking respect and recognize who the fuck you're talking to! Do I have to make a phone call, or are you gonna do what I say and get the fuck outta here?"

The bitch slap across their leader's face was all Juvie's goons needed to see. Immediately, they released Barkley from their clutches.

"Yo, Bark, you okay? You nodding yes, but I don't think you are. You know what I think would make you feel better? Punch one of these bitch ass niggas in their face. I'm telling you, it's a hell of a rush." Born took a step back and pointed towards Barkley's assaulters. "Okay, which one hit you first?"

"Nah, man it's cool. We get the point," Juvie said.

He barely finished his sentence before Barkley knocked him out cold with a flush blow to his chin.

"Oh, shit! I didn't even know you had that in you, son. I feel like Chris Tucker in *Friday*. He got knocked the fuck out!" Born said mockingly.

Barkley avoided a painful start to his day, but his encounter with Juvie would be just the beginning of a tumultuous day.

JAMAL A. BENJAMIN

Chapter 3

The ringing school bell prompted students to begin vacating the hallways inside Jackie Robinson High School and enter into their classrooms. Barkley entered his math class with the same excitement he would have if he were entering a jail cell. To Barkley, Mr. Monroe's math class felt like incarceration since this was the class that kept him off the school's basketball team. In his mind, Mr. Monroe made sure Barkley failed his class so his son could have a spot on the team. This thought consumed Barkley's mind making him feel uninspired and helpless. He knew his accusations of a conspiracy to keep him off the team would fall on deaf ears and cause more problems than solutions, so he kept it to himself.

"Mr. Capleton, are you with us today? I mean if you have other things to do like a parole hearing or a bodega to rob, don't let me keep you," Mr. Monroe snidely said.

The class erupted into laughter as Barkley and Mr. Monroe engaged in a stare down. Tension engulfed the room, which made some onlookers believe if either were holding a gun, murder would have been an easy act to commit. Barkley had finally reached his boiling point.

"I don't need this shit. Fuck you. Don't let me see you on the streets, and you better pray I don't see your son on the courts." Barkley said.

Mr. Monroe's comments gave him the gumption to do what he had been thinking about doing since he was kicked off the school's basketball team. Barkley left school. He walked out the door without a second thought of math class or any other class, ignoring Mr. Monroe's threats of suspension. The New York Public School system was now in his rearview mirror and there was no way he was entertaining the thought of making a U-turn. He wandered around for close to an hour before he encountered a friend he hadn't seen in a while.

Detective Shamus Harrison pulled up beside him in an unmarked car. It had been close to a year since the old friends saw each other. Thanks to his dedication to the Atkins diet, the Irish cop looked a lot healthier since he was no longer carrying as much weight. This was a new look for the New York police officer. It had been about a year since Harrison was promoted to Detective. At first glance Barkley had no clue who he was. With no other way to get his old friend to recognize him, Harrison bleeped the siren on his unmarked car to get Barkley's attention.

"And where the hell are you going? Last I checked school hours didn't end until about three o' clock and Jackie Robison High School ain't in the direction you're going," said Harrison.

When Barkley turned toward Harrison, streams of tears were flowing from his eyes. Seeing his young friend so upset immediately caused concerned and made him want find the root of his sadness. This encounter was unlike any he'd previously experienced with Barkley. They last saw each other when Barkley was shooting hoops in a Brooklyn park notorious for homeless drug fiends and shootings, during late night hours. It wasn't safe for a kid to be out there alone, and it was clear those dangerous surroundings were only going to cause harm if he stayed there. He tried to take him home, but the teen swindled the then beat cop into letting him stay on the court by challenging him to a game of H.O.R.S.E. It was during that contest, Harrison observed how special Barkley was on the basketball court. He hit amazing shots throughout the game. Again, he attempted to make the teen go home, but Barkley refused to go until Harrison beat him in a one-on-one match up. Since that meeting Barkley hadn't experienced any problems staying in the park after hours.

Harrison had never seen his young friend as sad as that day he saw Barkley walking away from his school. Barkley always had a smile when he the two crossed paths, but on that day there were too many negative thoughts running through his brain to form his customary grin.

"Hey, buddy, what's bothering you? You can tell me, man," said Harrison.

Barkley attempted to talk, but burst into tears before he could finish his sentence. As he cried he kept repeating the same comment.

"I can't do this anymore. I just can't do this shit. I can't."

"Hold on, buddy, hold on. What can't you do anymore? Are you in some kind of trouble? Whatever it is, we can deal with it. Me and you, nobody else. We can deal with it. Come with me. Don't worry, I'm not taking you back to school. We're gonna go somewhere to talk. Get in the car."

As Harrison drove off, he noticed that Barkley had started to calm down. There were plenty of questions he had, but there was no surefire way to go about getting answers. In an interrogation room, Harrison's dilemma would have ceased to exist. His interrogation methods were celebrated and revered. A few cops called him the Finisher, because once a perp sat down in that room under the light with Harrison, he was finished. The current situation with Barkley required more of a delicate approach. Harrison spent several minutes searching for words to console his friend, but none came to mind. He went with a direct approach but removed his renowned hard-edged demeanor.

"What's going on, man? Talk to me."

Holding back tears, Barkley began to share his entire life story for the first time. He told Harrison about the abandonment, violent attacks, adversity, and alienation. In the last twenty-four hours Barkley had revisited all four of those past experiences at once. And, with each passing hour, Barkley was reminded of the approaching date on which Mother Benson planned to kick him out, leaving him homeless with nowhere to go. Rough times throughout the years had hardened him, but he knew he didn't have the tough texture to survive on the streets for very long. He was scared and didn't know what he was going to do.

"Sometimes I don't even feel like living. I just wish I could ask God to change everything about me—my name, my life, my family, everything!" Barkley said.

As he was rubbing away the tears from his eyes, Barkley noticed Harrison's firearm in his unlatched holster and snatched it. Barkley put the gun to his own head.

"What the fuck are you doing?" Harrison yelled. He tried to grab the gun from Barkley, but lost control of the car and almost careened into a garbage truck. After he regained control, he pulled into an alley and focused on getting the gun away from Barkley. A brief tussle erupted as Harrison lunged toward Barkley to retrieve his firearm. The struggle to get back the gun abruptly ended when Barkley sprung up from his hunched over position and pointed the barrel at Harrison. There wasn't much that could startle Harrision, but Barkley's action left the seasoned veteran cop totally shocked. He had stared down the barrel of gun before, but a friend's finger on the trigger was definitely unchartered territory for him. Barkley didn't keep the nine-millimeter Berretta pointed at Harrison for long. After letting out a few heavy breaths, he shifted the gun to aim it his right temple.

"Bark, we go too far back for this. Talk to me, please. You've been through a lot. Shit, we all have, but you're not some weak bitch or a quitter. And what you're thinking about doing is quitting. Pulling that trigger is a weak move. You're on the edge, I know, but take a step back. We can do it together. Come on, man, you're not alone in this."

Barkley slowly started to take the gun down from his head and handed it to Harrison. Once the peaceful exchange was made, Barkley turned to look out the window. The stoic look on his face gave the impression he didn't care if there were repercussions from the chain of events that just transpired. During the ordeal Harrison held back from what he would normally do when a gun was pointed in his face. Barkley was his friend, so he didn't think to reach for his back-up piece holstered on his ankle. Now that his gun was back in his possession, there was no reason to coddle Barkley with kid gloves and he definitely wasn't going to hold his tongue.

"Do you know I could've fucking killed you? Or what if a blue and white came by on patrol and they see us tussling over a gun in an unmarked squad? Who do you think is getting lit up, huh? Huh!"

After avoiding a car wreck and averting a suicide attempt, some instant therapy was needed. Watching the waves crash on Coney Island beach always helped Harrison acquire some peace in his hectic and dangerous life. Harrison knew of fellow officers who found solace in drinking, women, drugs, gambling, and even crocheting, but he found his at the beach, so he took Barkley there.

"This is where I come to collect my thoughts and every time I come here I just let everything go. I walk on the beach and just yell." Barkley looked puzzled, so he continued. "Anything I fucking feel like yelling, that's what I shout. For instance, 'All women are bitches!' " he screamed, then chuckled. "Had some issues with the women I've been dating recently, you know?"

The release was refreshing, but it also drew some stares from the two elderly Jewish women passing by on the boardwalk. Barkley tapped his buddy to clue him in to his gaff.

"I don't give a fuck who is walking behind me. I'm a cop, so nobody's gonna fuck with me, especially two old fuckers who happen to be bitches!" Harrison yelled. "Now it's your turn."

Barkley closed his eyes, clenched his fist and screamed, "I hate this life! You motherfuckers trying to kill me. I don't give a fuck about you. You motherfuckers can't guard me. I want to take my dick and smack you with it. I wish I could stick a screwdriver up your ass, you bitches. Lick my nuts, you bitches!"

"Whoa, whoa! I think you filled your bitch quota for today, and honestly you talking about your dick and sticking objects up people's asses is a little discomforting," Harrison said.

In that moment, shouting to the heavens seemed to be the therapy Barkley needed. An hour later, Harrison pulled up at Barkley's home, officially ending the impromptu therapy session.

"You have some real issues that you have to deal with. This homeless situation is gonna work itself out. I know a few boarding houses where the owners owe me a favor, so if you need a place to stay I got you," offered Harrison.

Barkley exited the car feeling a lot better than he did when he originally got in. He took his time walking slowly up the stairs to his house, but as soon as he opened the door, Mother Benson could be heard cursing at his foster siblings, giving him a clear indication trouble was going to find him no matter what he did to avoid it.

JAMAL A. BENJAMIN

Chapter 4

On certain days Barkley would dribble his ball from his house all the way to school. It became common practice for people along the way to try to strip the ball away from him. It was pure amusement when the bums or other school kids would try to take the ball from him. However on this morning, his ability with the basketball would gain him access to an infamous figure in the neighborhood. When he left the house, Barkley didn't know where he was going. Since dropping out of school, he spent most days making small runs for Born. These drop-offs netted him some much-needed cash, but he wasn't going to make the kind of money he needed to support himself once he was kicked out of his foster home. Born didn't want a dead friend, so he wasn't going give him bigger jobs where it would have been a necessity to carry a gun. Barkley wasn't an official dropout, which meant getting some practice time in on playground courts was not an option because of the truancy officers on patrol. As Barkley dribbled his basketball toying with two neighborhood kids, a car pulled up and came to a screeching stop. The two kids trying to steal the ball from Barkley were startled and jumped back. Barkley kept his dribble and stared at the car with a look of brashness.

"I told you this nigga was nice," said Kevlar as he got out of the car.

Kevlar sat atop the food chain in Bed-Stuy's illegal pharmaceutical industry. His real name was name was Kevin Simmons. He earned his street moniker by surviving several attempts on his life. Kevlar suffered a total of ten gunshot wounds on five different occasions. His bullet-riddled body should have been in the morgue after each attempt on his life, but Kevlar managed to survive every time. It was as if he had on an invisible bullet-proof vest covering all of his major organs and arteries. He'd spilled plenty of blood on the streets of Brooklyn, but he was also responsible for leaving several people leaking on the ground.

"I bet my man fifty bucks he could pull up on you and you'd still keep your dribble. So I want to thank you, my nigga, for showing this punk that Bed-Stuy produces true ballers with heart. And of course making me some dough. Pay up, nigga," said Kevlar.

"Damn, don't I get some of that?" Barkley asked.

Kevlar looked at Barkley with a look of astonishment. "Oh, so I owe you something? Is that what you saying? Because if I do, by all means, speak up. I don't make a habit of owing people because, in my opinion, the word owe is derived from the word ownership, and there ain't a fucking person on this earth that own me. Now, do I owe you something?" asked Kevlar again as he stared at Barkley with a menacing look.

Barkley couldn't say a word. Anything he thought about saying didn't get the chance to leave his mouth because uttering those words never trumped his initial idea of keeping his mouth shut. Any response he had for Kevlar was overshadowed by his inner voice shouting, "Shut the fuck up!" The fact that this exchange with the baddest man on any block in Bed-Stuy was taking place during daylight hours did not give Barkley any comfort. He knew anything he uttered could be his last words.

"Damn, Kev, I need you around when my side chicks start asking me about money," his friend said.

"I'm just playing with this nigga right here. My man got too much talent for me to snuff him out on some bullshit like that. Man, you need a ride to school? Hop in. And speaking of getting paid, I got a business opportunity I think you might be interested in. Come on, man, hop in," Kevlar instructed.

With a combination of fear and hesitation, Barkley got into the car.

"I'm glad I saw you when I did because I was giving myself a fucking headache trying to decide who to give this golden ticket I got burning in my back pocket. For weeks I've been wondering if I should give this sweet ass opportunity to a local cat or outsource this job," Kevlar said.

Barkley's encounter with Kevlar was definitely not a chance meeting. The drug kingpin had a moneymaking venture lined up and needed one more component for his plan. He'd considered few other basketball phenoms in the neighborhood, but he specifically targeted Barkley.

"No disrespect, man, but I can't get down with the drug game. It's not me. Sooner or later the drug game turns into gun play, and just keeping it one hundred with you, I don't have the heart for those games," Barkley said.

Kevlar smirked at Barkley's honesty. He was overly amused by the delivery of Barkley's comments.

"So you'll shoot the rock, but you won't sell any. Is that what I'm hearing? My nigga, you narrow-minded motherfucker, just 'cause a nigga is in these streets twenty-four/seven don't mean I want to open up a 7-Eleven in this bitch. Just like you, I'm trying to get out of this 'hood, and I think I found a way out. I'm just trying to reach back into the community and take some niggas with me, but if you gonna slap my hand away, you can get the fuck out right now. Now are you ready to listen?" asked Kevlar.

The street life vet began his sales pitch with stories about his fatherless childhood and the hardcore life lessons that put him behind bars and in the line of fire of every stick-up kid and young corner hustler looking to make a name for himself. In recent years, Kevlar dreamed almost daily about getting out of the life. He finally drew up the blueprints for an escape plan one year ago to the day he crossed paths with Barkley. His plan called for the recruitment of the best street ballers to match up against teams in high stakes street ball gambling. Over the next two hours, Kevlar spoke of the crew of local playground basketball players he was giving a second shot at making something of their lives. The team traveled all along the east coast to play the top teams in every major city. He called his team BK To Tha Fullest. The moniker was a lyric from a Notorious B.I.G. song, which fit the team perfectly as they built a notorious reputation for embarrassing the competition in their own backyard. There were several people who wanted to connect the team with Kevlar's drug past, which made people, mainly law enforcement, think his new basketball venture was just a new vehicle for drug trafficking. With as much conviction as he could, Kevlar stressed to Barkley that there was nothing felonious about his team or anyone on it. BK To Tha Fullest was all about playing ball and beating the shit out of everybody they met on the court. He said he was offering Barkley a spot because one of his players just got an offer to play overseas.

"Who?" Barkley asked, wondering who from the 'hood was nicer than him.

"You know Kaseem Fields? Me and him go way back. I put him on my team and he was wrecking shit this past summer. In one game he caught this nasty dunk over Ron Artest at the Rucker. Two weeks later, the YouTube video of the dunk was featured on the top ten summer league dunks and landed on ESPN. No lie. Some team in Greece saw it and invited him for a tryout. Now my man is swimming in green and enjoying Greek pussy," Kevlar said.

His final sales pitch came in the form of dollars. Kevlar pulled out a wad of cash; stacks of Benjamins and Grants. It was more money than Barkley had ever seen. "I'm in!" he said.

"Now you know this means you gotta drop outta school right? I need a full-time b-baller because this is serious money we're playing for. We're not a professional team, but we handle our shit professionally. That means practice every other day, two games a week, and travel that keeps you outta town sometimes two weeks or more at a time. I don't want an answer now. Think about it and get back at me in a week. I'm all for school, but from what I hear and what I can see, it ain't doing shit for you and it damn sure ain't putting any green in your pockets."

Barkley was mesmerized by the amount of money Kevlar flashed before him and stopped staring only when Kevlar's car pulled up in front of the school he turned his back on just a few weeks earlier. Before he exited the vehicle, Barkley gave the cash one last stare down.

"What you waiting on, man? You got books to read. And I got paper to chase, so if you remember anything we talked about today you remember what Biggie said: 'You either sell rock or got a wicked ass jump shot.' This is your way to give a middle finger to all those that said you ain't shit and left your ass in the gutter," Kevlar said.

Barkley watched the Lexus SUV as if it was driving off with his last meal. He looked at his school then turned away to walk towards the basketball courts across the street.

Chapter 5

It had been nine months since Barkley decided to forgo education for hoop dreams, which did not cause him a bit of anguish or anxiety. Although he made the decision seconds after exiting Kevlar's ride, Barkley began to grow agitated and depressed over the waiting game Kevlar had him playing. A baby could have been born in the amount of time that passed. Unfortunately for Barkley, his new life was on an indefinite hold and he was very puzzled about it. Barkley hoped he could have gotten a response before he turned 18 so he could give Mother Benson his ass to kiss, but there was no form of communication from Kevlar. The little money he made with Born was enough to cover the monthly price tag placed on his room. Barkley wasn't home much. He spent most of the fall and winter months inside the local community center. The building's gymnasium became his second home where he honed his skills every day in anticipation of getting a call from Kevlar. Barkley dealt with disappointment his entire life and was very aware of the signs that would precede a new dosage of bitter pills he'd have to swallow, but this time was different. He had been waiting for a phone call for close to a year, but he still had hope.

When the last week in June rolled around, Barkley's hope started to diminish. It was summertime and street ball season was in full swing. This was when the best of the best resurfaced on some of New York City's best courts. Sightings of playground legends were reported daily at West 4th, Rucker Park, and The Kingdome. A hotbed of talent displayed their skills on the blacktop in every borough. On any given day, courts in Queens, Manhattan, Brooklyn, Staten Island, or The Bronx could become the stage for a virtuoso performance by at least two or three masters of street ball. Barkley witnessed these performances before, but he felt it was his time to showcase his talents. There wasn't a doubt in his mind, this summer was going to be his coming out party. The clock was about to strike midnight when he arrived home from a full day of practice and playing.

"Listen boy, just because you're paying rent don't mean you can come in here all hours of the night. If you can't come in before Conan O'Brien, keep yo' ass in the streets! You hear me? Answer me when I'm talking to you!" Mother Benson shouted.

Barkley walked past her as if she were invisible. Since making his decision, he'd only spoken few words to his foster family. He had found a way out and wasn't going to let any detractors or distractions get in his way. As he approached his room, he saw his three foster siblings huddled outside his door. Charity, Chase, and Kim were mumbling to themselves, each pushing the other to speak to Barkley first.

"Can you please get from in front of my fucking door?" Barkley asked.

"Oh, hell naw. He ain't got to curse at us. We are here to tell his mute ass something and he wanna start off by cussin' at us. I ain't the one. I ain't the one," Charity yelled.

"Bitch, say what you gotta say and leave me the fuck alone."

"Last I checked, bitches bark. They can't speak

English, so whatever it is I was meaning to tell you, like who called, I forgot how to say it. So woof, nigga, woof."

Barkley grabbed Charity and slammed her into a wall. He had every intention to do more, but when Chase yelled out that Kevlar called, Barkley stopped.

Chase quickly continued. "He said meet him at the park on Kingston and Atlantic at 9 a.m. sharp. Something like if you're late, you're out."

"You better not be fuckin' with me. No bullshit? Yeah! Yeah!" Barkley shouted.

His excitement could not be hidden even if he tried. He pulled Charity toward him and kissed her on the cheek. He even attempted to hug Chase.

"Nah, nigga, I'm good," Chase said.

"Keep that shit over there," Kim preemptively said.

Smiling ear to ear, Barkley entered his room and dove onto his bed. He began to daydream about winning games, driving fancy cars, and rolling through his 'hood with stacks of big faced Benjamins. This is what he had worked for since dropping out of school. The self-motivation to be great and find a way out of his personal hell-hole was now about to pay off. It was show time and Barkley was ready. The excitement about the morning meeting kept him from shutting his eyes as several thoughts and images crept into his head. He even likened this experience to what he thought it'd be like if he was at the NBA Draft waiting to hear his name called by commissioner, David Stern. In his fantasy, he wondered if Chris Paul, Kobe Bryant, and Lebron James felt the same kind of butterflies before they took their game to another level.

Aloud, Barkley wondered what nickname would be

bestowed upon him. "Oh shit! They gonna give me a nickname like all the greats. Future, Half Man Half Amazing, Bone Collector. They're probably going to call me Sir Bark. Nah, that sounds too old school and I'm all new school. Maybe Tree Bark, like dudes is barking up the wrong tree when they try to check me."

He imagined he had a ball and moved as if he were on the court. Using his imaginary ball, Barkley simulated every move he would make on the court over every inch of his room. Making up a nickname proved to be a daunting task. His efforts to create one that fit perfectly tired him out to the point of exhaustion. He spent over an hour racking his brain to come up with something as genius as Michael "Air" Jordan or Allen "The Answer" Iverson before collapsing on his bed. As Barkley drifted off to sleep, he felt confident about his skills. He had prepared himself for this day, and in his mind he was ready. There was no one on the planet that could guard him.

Beep, beep, beep! The clock read 8:30 a.m. It was time to get up. It was show time. Twenty-five minutes later, Barkley arrived at Carver Park. The local playground was desolate compared to how it was in past years. Most parents kept their children out of the park that had become fertile ground for gang activity and memorials for tragic losses of life. Barkley walked inside the park looking for Kevlar, but only saw an early morning baller shooting hoops. The man shooting hoops was an old school guy. He practiced hook shots and his spin moves that seemed to be straight out the 1970's Boston Celtics handbook.

"Hey, young fella, how about a l'il one-on-one to give this old man some exercise?" the stranger asked.

Barkley tried to ignore the middle-aged-looking

man's challenge, but he couldn't completely drown out the attempts to call him out.

"Hey! I'm talking to you. Yeah, you. Oh, we're being silent I see. How is this; I got one hundred bucks that says you can't score on me once."

Dollar signs were the kind of bait Barkley couldn't ignore. His attention was now squarely on the man waving the one hundred-dollar bill. Barkley gave the man a look of disbelief and began to walk towards him. As he got closer, Barkley noticed that the man was older than he initially thought. After spending hours in the gym, a David versus Goliath scenario was the first thought that came to Barkley's mind. The 6'1" lanky kid now had a muscular frame that made him look gigantic to the shorter and pudgy man offering the challenge.

"Are you serious? Times are tough; do you like losing money or something?" Without waiting for a response, Barkley continued, "So all I gotta do is score once?"

"I know I'm old, but I think I hear better than you. Isn't that what I said, youngster? No pull-up jump shot shit; take me to the hole. Earn your money." Before Barkley answered, the man introduced himself as Billy.

Barkley's aging adversary shoved the ball into his chest and the game was on. He tried to back down Billy, but the muscle he packed on wasn't helping against his rotund opponent. He was having a lot more difficulty than he thought he would. On top of that, he was being introduced to brutal a brand of basketball. Each move Barkley made was met by an elbow from Billy.

"Foul! Man, are you serious? That's not basketball," Barkley complained.

"Stop bitchin'," Billy said.

Play after play, Billy pulled out dirty tricks to stop Barkley from scoring. Barkley picked himself off the ground more often than he took shots. Bleeding from his mouth, Barkley decided he was gonna play the prison style ball Billy had just given him a crash course in. Barkley backed Billy down. As he spun away to take a jump shot Barkley faked his shot to get his defender in the air. With a smirk on his face, Barkley lead his shoulder into Billy's chest, effectively knocking him to the ground. Looking down at his adversary, Barkley leapt over him and yelled as he dunked the ball. Clapping his hands as he walked toward the court, Kevlar praised his young recruit,

"Well done! Well done, youngsta'."

"You were watching the whole time, weren't you?" Barkley asked.

"My research on my investments is never based off word of mouth or half-assed accounts of stories. It's an intensive process," Kevlar said.

It was a test, and Barkley passed with flying colors. He didn't quit and he didn't complain. To Kevlar, that represented heart and hunger. He knew Barkley's skill level, but he wanted to know if the kid had what it took to play in games that were more about talent than X's and O's. Barkley was on the team. His hard work and practice made him the newest member of BK To Tha Fullest, and now it was time for his coming out party. Kevlar invited him to the Casper Lounge to meet the rest of the team later that night. With a big smile and a stream of blood flowing down his face, Barkley left the park feeling like the prison gates were opening and there was nothing stopping him from grabbing all the fantasies he dreamed up. On his way home he bumped into his friend, Born.

"What the fuck? What happened to your face? Why is it every summer I got to fucking shoot somebody?" Born asked.

The smile across Barkley's face looked like it was rooted in insanity rather than the great news he'd just received. Born was almost spooked by the visual of his friend bleeding from his mouth and cheesing like he was about to take a photo.

"Man if you don't stop smiling and tell me what the fuck happened..." Born said.

Barkley calmed his friend down and told him his about his morning battle on the blacktop. Excitement was oozing from every pore of Barkley's being and every word he uttered. In the middle of his story, Barkley could tell his enthusiasm was not infectious. Born's blank stare did not change during any portion of the story.

"What's wrong with you, man? I tell you I'm about to make boo-koo bucks and get outta this fucking neighborhood, and you ain't happy for me? I'm rolling with Kevlar now, dog, you get it? I can walk these streets without a fucking care in the world. And did I mention I'm getting paid? I'm gonna be living the life. He's throwing a party for me tonight, so you gotta roll with me to the Casper," Barkley said.

Born's blank stare transformed into a look of anger. He pushed Barkley into a nearby fence and began to slap him in the head. "Is this it? Is this what I been protecting you for? So you can fucking slit your wrist? You just fucking killed yourself, you know that?" Born asked.

Barkley's smile turned into a look of fear. He'd never seen his friend this way. He'd known Born most of his life and thought he only had love for him—up until that point. Born continued his attack on Barkley and began to tell him about the Kevlar he knew. He spouted off stories about Kevlar's team that did not have a good ending. He told stories of players with limitless potential now living as paraplegics. His tales did not have the type of fairy tale endings Barkley envisioned for himself. Born's stories ended with players dead or dead broke.

"Now do you see why I'm so fucking angry? These streets, all aspects of them are the fucking underbelly of the beast and that life ain't for you, Bark. You got heart but you ain't got what it takes to survive in my world, in Kevlar's world."

Barkley leaned against the fence and slumped to the ground as if a few thousand pounds had been dropped on his shoulders. Looking like 50,000 volts had gone through his body, Barkley went dead silent, his mind consumed by thoughts of violence and death. He had come to the realization what he would do on the court would count more than any other basket he'd ever made. Barkley thought he had signed up for basketball, but on that day he learned the games he would be playing in were not about winning and losing. It was now about staying alive.

Chapter 6

It was 11:30 p.m. when Barkley showed up at the Casper Lounge. He paced back and forth on the corner across the street from the nightclub thinking about what it meant if he walked in. He questioned everything Kevlar told him. He questioned everything Born told him. Barkley thought about turning around and marching right back home. *It wouldn't be that bad.* He hadn't cost Kevlar any money. Several questions entered Barkley's mind, but the one he kept asking himself he already knew the answer to. Was he good enough to play with the best in the city? Born's tales were horrific and scary to think about, however, those stories were overshadowed by the thought of not playing, and that terrified him more than anything. Basketball was Barkley's Bible and the court was his sanctuary. He knew he had what it took to be great, and after thinking about it for a half hour, Barkley decided to sign his deal with the devil.

Walking into the Casper Lounge introduced Barkley into a world he'd never seen nor dreamed of being a part of. Wherever his eyes landed, he saw beautiful women dressed in attire that generated nothing but lust-filled fantasies. As he stepped further into the club, a nearby bouncer grabbed him.

"What's your young ass doin' in here? I can smell the breast milk on your breath, so get the fuck—"

The bouncer stopped and offered an apology in mid-sentence. Barkley turned to look over his shoulder and saw Kevlar. From that point on Barkley knew a life of excess awaited him. He walked past the bevy of attractive women stationed in front of Kevlar's table to greet his new boss.

"What the deal is, coach? Where is the rest of the team?" Barkley asked, looking around.

"Your teammates are around, but we'll get to that later. I'm not your coach. I'm more of a general manager/owner type. I'm also security when dumb motherfuckers need to be handled. Your coach is one of the best players I've ever seen and one of the best basketball minds you'll ever want to tap into," Kevlar said.

As Kevlar spoke, Barkley's eyes gravitated toward a non-shaven portly looking man walking in his direction. The dark circles under the man's eyes, his aging skin, and his graying hair easily made him look like the old dude in the club hunting young tail, but chasing pussy wasn't on the old timer's mind.

"Say what's up to your coach, Moncrief," Kevlar said to Barkley by way of an introduction.

"Yeah, young fella you got some heart, but when I get done with you, you're gonna have a brain to go with that heart," Moncrief said.

"Where's the rest of the team?" Barkley asked again.

"The only teammates you gonna meet tonight are these fine ladies standing right behind you. Tonight is your night, and we're gonna make sure you enjoy it, because after tonight it's all business," said Kevlar.

Before Barkley could say anything, two of the women approached him and put their arms around him. They started to rub his chest and the clouds of doubt floating in his head quickly evaporated. His dick told him he made the right decision walking into Casper Lounge.

"Now ladies this is my new point guard, so you treat him like his name Carmelo Anthony and his wife, LaLa, gave him a free pass to get fucked all night long," Kevlar said.

The two voluptuous women took Barkley upstairs to a bedroom in the back area of the club. They pushed him onto the bed and began to undress in front of him.

"You're gonna remember this for the rest of your life, baby," one woman said as she pushed play on the iPod dock.

From that moment everything played out in slow motion for Barkley. While one woman pulled down his the pants, the other started kissing on his neck and unbuttoning his shirt. Once his clothes were gone, both used their tongues to tantalize his body. As both women peppered the lower half of his body with kisses, they both noticed his erection at the same time. In a matter of seconds, two sets of lips were caressing the shaft of Barkley's penis. His body trembled and a tear streamed from his left eye. His eyes rolled backward as the incredible pleasure stemming from his first oral experience consumed his entire body. He felt teased when the women paused to blindfold him. He was rewarded for his patience when he was straddled by the sexiest ass he'd ever felt in the palm of his hands. While one woman showered Barkley with kisses on his neck and back, the other rode him clinching every inch of his penis with her vaginal muscles as she thrust her waist back and forward. He did his best to keep his mind off of climaxing, but the explosion of semen was inevitable. Once he came, embarrassment consumed him, but sensing his inexperience, his two paramours consoled him.

"It's okay, baby, we got all night," one woman said. As he lied in the bed with both women in the fetal position under his arms, Barkley worried if his second sexual experience would be delayed for another night. He had never experienced an orgasm, and as the women stroked his leg, the blood in his body began to rush to his lower half. *Ding, ding,* he was ready for round two.

Barkley woke up the next morning with both women draped over his legs. Moncrief sounded like he wanted to tear the door down each time he battered the door with his knocks. He couldn't help but laugh as he walked into the room and saw the look on Barkley's face.

"You looked like a scared puppy when these fine ass ladies were escorting you up here. But now look at ya, looking all manly and shit. Let's hope these two didn't suck and fuck all the energy out of you, because we got a game, young fella'. Uh-huh. Kevlar set it up last night. Big bucks, man. He must think you're something special because he's putting up fifty thousand and has a side bet of twenty thousand on you to outscore their point guard. His name is…what's his damn name? I'm always forgetting shit. Uh, Mellow Man! Yeah, that's him!" Moncrief said.

"Mellow Man! That dude is a playground legend," Barkley said.

"And you'll be one too if you do what I tell you and play smart. Now get out of this damn bed. We got a game. It's 6 p.m. at the Kingdome. I'll see you there at five. And the best advice I can give you is don't fuck with Kevlar's money. We win, he's happy. We lose, and that is a shit storm you don't want in your forecast," Moncrief said.

He reminded Barkley not to be late because the

Kingdome got crowded early, and with a wager in the thousands, the night was sure to be electric. As instructed, Barkley arrived on time. This was the first time he met his teammates, and he wanted to impress them, but as soon as he arrived, there was an immediate stare down. There was no way he was backing down.

"You guys need to stop eye fucking each other and say hello, damn it, so we can get down to business," Moncrief said.

"What's up, young fella? Let's get this paper," Man Child said. His burly 6'8" figure made him look more like an NFL lineman than a basketball center. He was definitely the enforcer of the team, and his job was to clog the middle and clothesline anybody that tried to come down the lane. Khakalak introduced himself next. The country boy could shoot the lights out. There wasn't a spot on the court where he couldn't hit his jump shot. With his 6'2" slender frame you wouldn't think he was a baller because he had no muscle tone, one of the longest heads known to man, and he didn't seem like he belonged on any courts in the Big Apple. Nonetheless, he'd made a name for himself on the courts of Raleigh, North Carolina. Kevlar saw him play in one game and brought him to the city. Barkley's final two teammates were Double-Double. The twin brothers played guard and forward. Off the court, they could not agree on or share anything but women. Although they were on the same team, there was always a competition between them. It didn't matter what it was, both would try to outdo one another on every possible occasion. Their competitiveness was always high, since both stood toe-to-toe at 6'5" with rippling muscles. After all of the greetings took place, Moncrief gave the team their game plan. It was a simple game plan that only required three words: bust their asses!

As the teams walked toward center court, the crowd erupted with shouts and applause, creating an atmosphere that was unlike anything Barkley had experienced. His adversary for the day, Mellow Man was known for his dribbling ability. He'd embarrassed quite a few people at the Kingdome. Mellow Man's team, Franklin Towers, was known for its dirty play and high-flying dunks. They'd never lost at the Kingdome, and getting a win there meant slaying what seemed to be a three-headed monster. Franklin Towers came there to win. The crowd wanted Franklin Towers to win. And although the refs were supposed to be a neutral element of the game, Barkley and his teammates knew they wouldn't be.

Barkley positioned himself for the jump ball across from Mellow Man at center court. Before the ball was thrown up, he spotted a familiar face in the crowd. It was Born. Spotting a friendly face was just the confidence booster he needed. In that instance, all of the nervousness and anxiety festering inside him vanished. He was now certain of his abilities and focused on what he was going to do. And that was win the game.

At halftime the score read, "FRANKLIN TOWERS-45, BK TO THA FULLEST-38." The teams were evenly matched, but the referees swallowed their whistles when it came time to call a foul on Franklin Towers for most of the game's first half. Just as Barkley and his teammates predicted, they were going to have to fight an uphill battle to win this game. The buzzer sounded for the second half to begin. As Barkley walked onto the court, Kevlar pulled him aside.

"What the fuck did I bring you in here for? You're playing like a l'il bitch. Mellow Man ain't got shit on you and you're letting him skate on you like his name is *Disney On Ice*. Get your game up. Get your fucking game up!" Kevlar said. If his words didn't express the seriousness of the situation, the shove to the court instantly delivered the message.

Mellow Man caught a glimpse of Barkley's tongue lashing from Kevlar, and decided to throw his own verbal jabs. "I see why you don't have no mama or daddy. The way I'm busting your ass I wouldn't claim your ass either," Mellow Man said.

The comment came from an insignificant source, but those words hurt Barkley to his core. It reminded him of the feeling of worthlessness he felt each time he woke up. The darkness that consumed his life. The darkness that was only lifted when he would set foot on a basketball court. The combination of those emotions exploded in his mind. He dropped to his knees and stared at the ground. Most onlookers thought he was about to start praying to Allah since at first glance he resembled a Muslim in a deep prayer. His teammates and the opposing team watched Barkley waiting to see what he would do. As if he was resurrected, Barkley hopped to his feet with a look of determination that made the baby faced teen look like a man on a mission. The referee blew the whistle for the second half to begin. On his first trip up the court Barkley drove straight at Mellow Man and pulled up at the top of the key for a three pointer. *Swish!* Mellow Man had the same objective in mind. Barkley would have none of that. He stripped the ball from Mellow Man. With a clear lane for a lay-up, Barkley pulled up for a shot just outside of the arc for another three pointer. *Swish!* With the ball in his hand, Barkley played at a skill level that was well above his adversaries. On defense he locked up a playground legend that was used to working magic with the ball. Against Barkley, Mellow Man's normal playground ball tricks turned into duds. Every move Mellow Man made, Barkley had a response for. As the game progressed, the spectators and the announcers began to notice what was happening before their eyes. Barkley's time had arrived. The first tale of street basketball's newest phenom was being written at the expense of one of the greats. The hostile crowd that was present at the beginning of the game had all of sudden shifted to the other side. Each time Barkley got the ball, the crowd would rise to its feet. They knew they were witnessing something special. Barkley did not disappoint. The roar of the crowd could be heard from blocks away.

"Oh my God, he is killing them," one spectator said.

"This kid is the truth," another chimed in.

There was more colorful commentary on Barkley's play provided by the play-by-play/hype man of the game shouting from the scorer's table.

"Who is this kid? Uh-oh! Uh-oh! They givin' him the ball again. He pulls up. Money! Dinero! This kid is definitely young moolah."

Almost instantly the crowd picked up on Barkley's new name. The DJ spinning songs began to mix in Lil Wayne screaming "Young Moolah, baby!" each time Barkley took a shot. From that point on, each time he took a shot, the *crowd* would yell, "Young Moolah, baby!" He didn't make every shot, but he made enough to lead his team to victory. Eighty-five to seventy was the final score. After the game, Barkley's teammates, Double-Double, lifted him onto their shoulders as the crowd applauded and cheered. Barkley had no problem immersing himself in the celebration of his performance. He could hear people talking about him as they left the park. The story behind that game would be told in various ways, but the one constant storyline would be the emergence of Young Moolah.

JAMAL A. BENJAMIN

Chapter 7

After the game, the team met Kevlar at the Casper Lounge. Each player was met with hugs, kisses, and congratulatory comments on their win, but Barkley was clearly the superstar. Kevlar pulled Barkley to the side for a chat. Kevlar didn't smile much so Barkley did not know what to expect, even after a win.

"I'm only gonna say this once. If you ever play like that again, you're gonna make me very...." Kevlar paused for a moment, looking into Barkley's eye with a very stern look. "A very rich motherfucker. Now let's pop some motherfucking bottles," Kevlar said as he laughed and embraced Barkley.

After about an hour of drinking, Barkley, Moncrief, and Khakalak were the only members of team that remained inside Casper. All three were experiencing a nice buzz thanks to the large amount of booze running through their systems. Kevlar and the rest of the team had left the lounge twenty minutes earlier. Barkley wanted to know what kind of lifestyle and experiences he could expect from playing with the team. He knew what it was like to win and the rock star treatment that comes with it. Now he wondered what it would be like if the team lost. Barkley knew most people on the wrong side of a high stakes bet wouldn't take too kindly to losing money, especially if there were thousands of dollars on the line. Moncrief was slumped over in his chair snoring, so he couldn't ask the person with the most knowledge on the topic. Without seeming like he was prying too much, Barkley began to talk to Khakalak with hopes of getting answers to some of his questions. Within five minutes, Barkley knew that was a bad decision. He'd only got one question in.

"So do you miss the South, Khak?"

"Hell yeah, I miss the South," Khakalak replied.

The southern country boy was an encyclopedia of information on everything that was ghetto, ratchet, and below the Mason Dixon line, like breakfast at Chick-Fil-A, late night runs to the Waffle House, ass clapping strippers, and buying rims on lay-a-way. Ten minutes had passed before Barkley could get in another question.

"So how did you hook up with Kevlar?"

Khakalak chuckled to himself. He poured the remainder of the Grey Goose into his glass. He looked at it for a moment before stroking all of the contents back in one motion. Khakalak's face grimaced as the vodka traveled down his throat. He took a deep breath and began his story.

He was a high school stud in a small town outside of Greenville, South Carolina. Like so many other young boys growing up in poor neighborhoods, he thought putting the ball in the basket was the perfect remedy for his family's poverty. All he did was play basketball. Khakalak consumed a daily diet of jump shots, dribbling exercises, and conditioning. His father, Giant, was the driving force behind his basketball aspirations. Standing 6'6" and weighing 275 pounds, Giant didn't need to say much to get his point across. Calling him an imposing figure would be an understatement. His glory days with the South Carolina Gamecocks made him a hero to black folks throughout several neighborhoods in and around Greenville. However, his side hustle made him a villain in the eyes of a few seedy characters. On the surface, he was just a UPS delivery man who got up every morning to make an honest living. Digging a little deeper revealed a violent individual who moonlighted as muscle for some of the local drug dealers. In South Carolina's world of illegal narcotics, he was an undeniable force to be reckoned with and Fort Knox-like security if you wanted to move product through the state. In search of a better price on product, Kevlar turned up at one of Khakalak's high school games. Kevlar and Giant became fast friends. For the first few hours they didn't talk about any type of deals. They only talked about basketball. As they debated about Jordan and Kobe, the talk shifted to Khakalak. Giant spoke of his son's potential and dreams of him making it to the NBA. From that first meeting, Giant and Kevlar forged a very lucrative relationship for both. Kevlar began to make trips down south on a monthly basis, and each time he came to town, he made a point to catch one of Khakalak's games. The relationship between Khakalak and Giant went sour almost three years to the day they initially met. From what Khakalak remembered, he said Kevlar put together a summer basketball team with the intentions of making him the star player. Giant put the kibosh on Kevlar's plan because he didn't want his son in New York. Kevlar offered to fly him back and forth, but Giant still refused because such an act would jeopardize his son's eligibility for a scholarship at a Division 1 program. Kevlar tried to convince Giant to let Khakalak come to New York for one game, but the protective father refused. The disagreement between Giant and Kevlar escalated to a heated argument when Giant mentioned Kevlar's attempt to extract some of his muscle from his crew. Giant didn't trust northerners very much. He felt they didn't honor the sanctity nor appreciate the true value of family. Giant often criticized Kevlar about his misunderstanding of southern values. Although he was a monthly visitor, Kevlar could never comprehend the loyalty crews showed each other in the south. The conversation did not net him the deal he was seeking, but he did learn a lesson about the impenetrable family bonds that could be found throughout the south, There was no fear of snitching or a rat weaseling his way in because family didn't take on those roles in Giant's brood. The heated exchange escalated when the subject matter turned toward Kevlar's alleged attempt to siphon resources from Giant's rank of street soldiers.

"When you talk to Rugby, you talking to me and vice versa. So how the fuck you gonna try to get one of my lieutenants to leave me to go up north with you? That shit is a fucking insult. You didn't think he would tell me all the shit you offered him and all the shit about me not taking him seriously or not caring about his needs? I should've cashed you out after hearing that shit, but now you going after my boy, and for him I will definitely kill," Giant said.

The awkward silence that followed served as a precursor to the dissolution of the pair's lucrative relationship. With not much to say after that, both men agreed not to do business with each other anymore.

As both were getting into their cars, gunfire erupted. A black Cadillac Escalade raced by, blasting bullets in Kevlar and Giant's direction. A cascade of AK-47 shells showered from the vehicle as the gunmen fired, leaving Kevlar's and Giant's cars riddled with bullet holes. The assassination attempt paved the street with shattered glass and blood. Once the bullets stopped flying, Kevlar heard the killers' getaway car roar down the roadway. With bullet wounds in his right arm and left leg, he crawled over to

Giant's lifeless body. Since both were seedy characters, authorities didn't put too many hours behind investigating who the assassins were targeting. There was one less drug dealer in their neck of the woods, and that's all they cared about. Kevlar was hospitalized for almost a week before he returned to New York. Left with no dad and a mom who'd passed from an overdose one year after his birth, Khakalak was alone. Upon hearing the news of his dad, Khaklak began a downward spiral. It wasn't too long before he dropped out of school. He was numb to the world and dead inside. The family Giant spoke so passionately about didn't carry the same convictions when it came to loyalty and caring for his son. Kevlar never returned to South Carolina until Khakalak hit his lowest point. After dropping out of school, Khakalak began to live a life destined to come to a violent and tragic conclusion. He lived off the money his father stashed in the house until he was robbed. His father's line of work was all he knew other than basketball, but Khakalak was not cut from the same durable fabric as his dad. Giant's name and the countless favors he granted generated a few dollars here and there for Khakalak, but it did not grant him a pass when it came to the laws of the streets. He developed a bad habit of not paying people back. Rugby did his best to help Khakalak after his father died, but he could only do so much for someone who did not want to be helped. Rugby's patience with Khakalak ended when he stiffed a small time pimp on the one hundred-dollar price tag attached to the pussy he spent one night pounding. It hurt his heart to do it, but Rugby gave the green light to take out Khakalak. It was his way of putting his old friend's offspring out of his misery. For weeks, Khakalak hid out at different places to avoid the bullet with his name on it. A crew of Rugby's enforcers finally caught up with Khakalak as he arrived at the home of a former girlfriend. Three men pulled up in a minivan with dark tinted windows. Two jumped out and threw him into the vehicle. Tied up and muzzled, Khakalak could only think he was taking his last breath. He was deep in prayer when the car came to a stop at a deserted farm. The men dragged Khakalak from the back of the car and tossed him forward. He landed at the feet of two men and closed his eyes and waited for his life to end.

"You sure you want this piece of shit?" Rugby asked.

Khakalak turned over onto his back to see Rugby standing next to Kevlar. He'd returned to South Carolina after hearing of Khaklak's slow demise. The trip down south didn't come without risks. Kevlar's wounds from the drive-by shooting were nothing more than bullet grazes. His small scale injuries made many think he was the one who orchestrated the hit on Giant, but there was never any proof.

"I don't ever wanna see this motherfucker in my 'hood again or else his ass is gonna be performing a disappearing act that's gonna be very fucking painful, you feel me?"

"You got it man," Kevlar said.

Still confused as to what was going on, Kevlar explained to Khakalak that his debt had been paid in full and the only issue he now had was figuring out how he was going to repay him for putting up the money. Before, Khakalak could say a word, Kevlar told him he had some ideas and that they would talk about it on the way to New York.

By the time Khakalak reached that portion of his story Barkley had grown a little agitated. The combination of Grey Goose and Khakalak's long winded storytelling began to take its toll. His bed was calling but he wanted to hear the conclusion of Khakalak's story. He attempted to help his teammate bring the story to a close by asking one question Barkley was very interested in finding out the answer.

"Do you still owe him?"

"Nah, it took some time, but I really just love New York, man. Bringing me here was the best thing for me. I got a guy coming to look at me the next game for an overseas gig. That would have never happened in South Carolina, and if Rugby didn't come after me, somebody else would have. Kevlar saved my life. And for that I owe him everything."

The two teammates finished the bottle of Grey Goose and headed out the door.

"C'mon man, let's go to the Golden Lady. It's Stripper Idol night. I got you, young buck. Your first lap dance is on me, but just make sure you don't choose any of the bitches with bullet wounds on their ass."

JAMAL A. BENJAMIN

Chapter 8

It was a month into the summer and Kevlar's team had a very lucrative winning streak, which put some buzz behind Barkley. His name was being mentioned when fans and old timers began discussing the next crop of street ball legends. Talk about the new point guard Kevlar found was circulating throughout the city's hottest basketball havens. The buzz did not go to Barkley's head, but he walked with a little more confidence and swag now that he was stuffing bundles of cash into his pockets after every game. Since BK To Tha Fullest had not lost a game yet, getting the reputation of a sure bet became catnip for the gamblers. The growing attention generated more cash at the games. The take home pay for BK To Tha Fullest after Barkley's first game was fifty thousand dollars. Splitting five figures between the team gave each player a nice bulge in their wallets, but as the wins stacked up, that pot of fifty thousand seemed like small potatoes compared to the rewards Barkley and his teammates were playing for now. After the third game, the team did not play for any amount less than seventy-five grand. Kevlar would get seventy percent of the winnings since he was putting up the money for the game. Thirty percent split between five players did not afford Barkley the kind of money to move into a life of luxury, but he did make enough to enjoy some good times and bring along a friend for the ride.

It was 11 p.m. on a Saturday night when a black Lincoln Town Car pulled up to the corner Born called his drugstore. In the corner of his eye, Born saw the rear window on the driver's side begin to come down. He noticed a black object slowly creeping out. Without hesitation, Born pulled his gun and pointed it toward the car.

"Whoa, whoa! It's just Moet, my dude. Man you was about to kill the best night you'd ever have in your life, and me in the process," Barkley said as the bubbly showered the street corner.

It had been a while since Barkley had seen his old friend and protector. It was not a peaceful parting of ways the last time they spoke and Barkley wanted to make things right. He was gonna start by treating his buddy to a night on the town.

"C'mon man, this ride to Manhattan is all paid for. We can go to Harlem Lanes, get some bowling in, talk to some chicks, get drunk, get thrown out. Growing up we never had a chance to do anything like this. Now it's our time and it's long overdue," Barkley said as he fanned himself with hundred-dollar bills. Born walked toward the car, but before he got in, Barkley told him to leave his gun. "You won't need that where we're going tonight, but you will need some Magnums. Oh, I forgot, you need the little dick condoms."

Born threw up his middle finger to Barkley and handed his gun to his drugstore co-owner before he got in the car. The two friends headed to Harlem for a night of fun, drinking, reminiscing, and laughing until they reached the bowling alley. Barkley and Born had a buzz that had them floating on air. As they entered the establishment's lounge area, an assortment of beautiful women with big asses wearing skirts and short shorts were spotted at every turn. They looked at each other and smiled, knowing the real party was about to start. The two friends begin with a shot of Absolut vodka and quickly graduated to shots of Patron. Hip-hop beats blared from the speakers as the grown and sexy vibe consumed the room. Born and Barkley were about to take their fifth shot when they noticed a voluptuous woman with a sexy Halle Berry-style hair cut walking their way.

"It looks like the party is over here," the caramel-complexioned hottie said.

They both stared at her, eyes locked on her cleavage. In her southern accent, she asked to join the fellas for a drink.

"Hell no," Born said.

"Now, don't be rude, my brother. Let's see what the lady is about first. For example, what's your name? Never mind, I don't need all that info just yet. Tell me this: you look like a woman with expensive tastes. Am I right?"

She nodded, and Barkley continued. "Good. We would get along great because my dick is worth a million dollars."

The woman nudged Barkley and angrily left the lounge area.

"Hey, bitch, don't be shoving people; he fights girls too," Born said.

The laughs and the liquor kept coming as the night progressed. In between the jokes, the two old friends reflected on their lives and where they thought they were going. Born talked about his life on the streets and the comfort he felt living day to day and not thinking about the future. His low self-esteem and lack of confidence in himself made him fertile ground for destructive behavior. Barkley had a different idea of what he wanted his life to be like. He talked of playing professionally and putting his haunting past behind him. It was a few minutes past 4 a.m. when the last drop of vodka was consumed. Each with one arm around the other, Barkley and Born stumbled out of the lounge to look for a cab, then walked a couple of blocks further to a more busy intersection with the hopes of increasing their chance of being picked up. The massive alcohol consumption made Born's legs feel like Jello, and after two blocks, they felt completely numb, causing him to fall face first onto the concrete.

"Damn, my dude. Move your fuckin' feet. Right, left, right, left," Barkley said. He helped Born onto his feet and looked into his eyes to see if he was conscious. Barkley repeatedly asked his friend if he was alright, but didn't get an answer. Born finally gave a response, but it wasn't one Barkley expected. He put both hands on Barkley's shoulder and leaned forward to attempt a kiss. Shocked by his friend's advance, Barkley stepped back and pushed Born away from him.

"What the fuck was that?" Barkley asked.

With slurred speech, Born began to apologize profusely to his friend.

"I'm sorry. I'm sorry, my nig. I didn't...I didn't..." Born said.

He continuously apologized until he began vomiting on the corner of 125th Street and Adam Clayton Powell Blvd. Once his river of vomit ran dry, Born burst into tears. Barkley watched and listened as his best friend explained the torture associated with hiding his sexuality. The daily demons he faced were unlike any Barkley had heard of or suspected from Born. He spoke of men he had bedded. He even spoke of men he sentenced to death by having unprotected sex.

"I've had the bug for about three years now. These streets have taken so much from me so why should I give a fuck if I shoot some poison back into them?"

He didn't know how many people he infected with HIV, but the guilt was beginning to take its toll on him. There were several times the idea of counseling crept into his head, but the dangers associated with rumors circulating about his gay lifestyle proved to be a great deterrent to therapy. Barkley was unsure of what his friend wanted from him. He knew he wasn't going to be providing any happy endings—or beginnings for that matter. Born knew Barkley wasn't gay, but making an advance was the best way to bring his deep secret to the surface. He'd thought about telling Barkley for some time but did not know the words to use, or how to tell his friend about the man he truly was. Once his friend completed the purging of his soul, Barkley could think of nothing but holding his friend. He hugged him and he held tight. That is how he wanted to translate his acceptance to his old friend. He also gave him some advice.

"You gotta get outta town man. Just leave this street life in the rearview. All that shit is gonna catch up with you. I got some dough and with the amount you got stashed you can make a new start somewhere," Barkley said.

Born had protected Barkley for years and felt an obligation to protect him from any threats he faced on the streets, but in the process, he could never look in the mirror to see the carnage he was creating by poisoning the community with narcotics spreading addiction and AIDS. Although he always thought of leaving the city, his monstrous ways would not play so well in less rugged areas of society. There was also a time when leaving would have meant rougher times for Barkley, and Born took it upon himself to make sure that didn't happen. Things were different now. Barkley was growing up and getting the street smarts that had eluded him for years. He didn't need his big brother like he had in the past. He put Born in a cab and began to walk towards the A train. It was long way to Brooklyn with many dangers lurking, but Barkley knew it was time to take that ride and begin a life without Born.

Barkley did not know where Born was headed nor did he want to know after they parted ways. He just knew he had to help his friend free himself from the shackles the streets had placed on him, and that meant removing himself from the list of concerns in Born's life.

Chapter 9

The buzzer went off, signifying the end of the game. The cheers coming from the crowd and Lil Wayne shouting "Young Moolah, baby" from the DJ's speakers meant one thing: Barkley had just put on a show and led his team to another victory. That was ten straight. Barkley was definitely enjoying the winning streak. He was getting approached by kids for autographs and by women with aspirations to fuck the city's newest street ball star. Amid the fanfare, Barkley noticed Kevlar talking to a man seated next to him. This was a white man Barkley remembered seeing somewhere, but could not remember where exactly. Kevlar and the man approached him. Both of the men smiled and embraced Barkley.

"Barkley, this is my man, Angelo, and he is gonna make us a lot of money," Kevlar said.

At first glance, Angelo did not come across as a high roller. He was dressed in a simple solid red T-shirt, white headband, blue jean shorts and retro Air Jordans. Unlike most of the people who came up to Barkley, Angelo was short on the complimentary talk. He was all business. He talked about putting major money on Bk To Tha Fullest against a professional Russian team. This game was a serious investment for Angelo, and he made it clear anything but a win was unacceptable. This was one of the times Barkley missed Born. He'd seen Angelo before but he could not remember where. Born knew all the players, and if he didn't know them, he had the ability to find out who they were and what kind of connections they had. After

64

giving himself a headache trying to figure out where he'd seen Angelo before, Barkley dropped it. Later, he joined Kevlar and the rest of his teammates at Casper Lounge and talked about their next game. Everyone on the team was buzzing with excitement. Barkley and his teammates openly exchanged thoughts about getting contract offers and playing ball overseas after handing the Russian team an old fashioned American-style ass whipping like the one Rocky gave Ivan Drago. Kevlar let the guys immerse themselves in the excitement of the moment. He let it last for a good five minutes before he dropped the hammer on their dreams. The team fell silent after Kevlar slammed his hand on a nearby table. He had their attention. Kevlar knew his guys could mop the floor with the Russian team, but vengeance was on his mind. Kevlar gathered the team in the back of Casper Lounge and began to tell them the back story of his relationship with Angelo.

They initially met through a mutual friend at the Kat Back Gentleman's Club. Midway through a night of boozing and smacking asses at the New Jersey strip club, Kevlar noticed the amount of cash Angelo was spending. He was intrigued and bought him a lap dance. This was all in an effort to get to know the white boy with all the money. Angelo was very appreciative of Kevlar's gesture and the two of started to talk. The light conversation turned into business when Angelo learned Kevlar had both feet planted in the drug game. Kevlar had access to whatever Angelo needed, but Angelo did not want to buy anything. He wanted to make a sale. He had a large stock of steroids he wanted to get rid of. In Kevlar's world he did not come in contact with too many 'roid-ragers, but the deal made sense to him. Kevlar would make the transaction now and have a favor owed to him in his back pocket for later. The deal went over without a problem. Both parties walked away satisfied and agreed to do more business in the future. Kevlar did not have any plans to unload the steroids until he was approached with a business plan concocted by a close relative. His beloved nephew is the family member who changed his thinking on the performance enhancing drugs.

Kevlar cared for Christian as if he was his own son. He helped his sister raise her only child and went to great lengths to make sure Christian had all the tools to lift himself up and away from the pitfalls awaiting black males in Bed-Stuy Brooklyn. Among receiving the best schooling Kevlar's money could buy and the latest fashion and accessories desired by teens nationwide, Christian was the focus of a collective effort spear-headed by his mom and uncle to keep the teen off the streets and away from the gravitational pull associated with fast money and the violence that snatched the lives of many black children every year. A few weeks before Kevlar made the deal, Christian began his freshman year at the University of Massachusetts. Similar to most first year college students, Christian had a difficult time fitting in. Girls did not like him because he wasn't a jock. The jocks didn't like him because of his cocky New York City attitude. Being treated like a leper was not an experience Christian was accustomed to. He was ready to drop out until he got wind of his uncle's steroid transaction. Kevlar's steroid shipment was gathering dust until his nephew opened his eyes to the fortune he was sitting on. Christian came up with a plan to sell the steroids to guys on the football team. The idea was a guaranteed money-maker, but the cash wasn't the real prize Christian had his eyes on. The dead presidents were going to make the weekends a lot more fun, but the new revenue stream was also going to put Christian on the fast track to the popularity and attention he primarily coveted. Reluctantly, Kevlar agreed to let his nephew have the stockpile of steroids. Everything was going as Christian had planned. He made the sales, and was immediately embraced. His acceptance lasted less than a week. His mangled body was found in a wooded area about a mile away from the location of a frat party he attended. Police investigators closed the case as a hit and run. There was enough evidence to support the notion of an intoxicated kid being struck by a car as he ran along a dark back road. The story even made sense to Kevlar until he answered a phone call at his sister's home. The caller could barely control his emotions as he told the story of what really happened to Christian.

The Kappa Alpha Chi house party was jumping. Sex, drinking, and drug use were rampant throughout the house. Christian was totally unaware of the storm coming his way. A forewarning wouldn't have done any good. The popular new kid was getting attention from some of the hottest co-eds on campus and he indulged every chance he got. That fateful night was no different. Christian was engaging in a wild episode of alcohol-induced sex when members of the football team entered the party looking for him. The crowd of students parted like the Red Sea and pointed in the direction of the room where Christian was laying the pipe to a redhead Asian chick he'd just met thirty minutes prior. The three burly defensive linemen kicked in the door, stunning Christian.

"You sold us bullshit," one of the football players

said.

"What are you talking about?"

"This shit ain't steroids. Saline solution isn't gonna help me keep my spot on the team, you fucking jungle bunny," the football player said as he threw a beer bottle in Christian's direction.

Fearing for his life and with no exit other than the window, Christian leaped out. He was on the first floor, so he was able to make a run for it after getting up from his fall. Dressed in only his underwear, Christian ran toward the road. Luckily for him, these were linemen chasing him, so he did not have to worry about them catching up to him quickly. He continued to look behind him as he ran toward the road. His attention was fixated on the world of hurt that he would be subjected to if he got caught. So he did not notice the car driving toward the direction he was running. As he ran, Christian took one last look behind him to see if his pursuers were nearby. He was in the clear, but in front of him was death. Just as he turned to look in front of himself, a Ford Explorer plowed into him on the dark road. The driver of the SUV waited for a while then drove off. Christian heard screams and multiple shouts for someone to call 911 before he lost consciousness and died. The caller ended the story by telling Kevlar no one wanted to kill the futures of the three football players who went after Christian that night, so a story was cooked up that everyone agreed to.

Consumed by rage, Kevlar hurled the phone into the wall and walked out of his sister's home. He paced back and forth, with thoughts of revenge on his mind. His initial thought was to find the football players and riddle their bodies with bullets from every gun he possessed. He then remembered where all of the troubles for his nephew began. Angelo. It was Angelo's signature on his nephew's death certificate. It was Angelo who was now going to experience unbearable pain to the point where he pleaded for his own death. Angelo was already dead in Kevlar's mind, but he knew going on a crazed rampage to kill a well-connected white boy was a suicide mission. This wasn't some nigger on the street that no one was going to miss. Putting a bullet in Angelo was always a part of Kevlar's plan, but he also wanted to embarrass him. When Angelo resurfaced with an offer Kevlar could not refuse, it was the perfect opportunity to put a few holes in him, but first he wanted to make back the cash Angelo stole from him. Because of his team's performance on the court, Kevlar was rolling in money. His name would surface immediately if you were looking for a big money game. Kevlar's name also crept into high stakes gambling circles. Angelo's addiction to gambling made him a permanent resident inside that world. He was a staple at events where the reward was great, but the risk of losing was greater. Angelo bet on everything. He placed wagers on dog fighting, horse racing, professional sports, collegiate sports, and pee-wee football. There was even a story of him betting on a schoolyard race he stumbled upon one morning after a night of heavy drinking and celebrating a bet he had won. His infatuation with choosing the underdog and making large bets against the odds made others think he had an appetite for destruction. But there was a method to his madness that no one could figure out. His betting patterns became legendary. They were legendary because he rarely lost.

    The initial meeting where Angelo reconnected with

Kevlar took place a couple weeks prior to when the team was informed about the revenge plot. Kevlar was at the Kat Back Club celebrating his team's ninth consecutive victory when he saw the man he had been fantasizing about killing. Angelo walked into the club with a couple of buddies and walked straight toward Kevlar. The men invited Kevlar to the VIP section and offered to take care of his bill. Kevlar could barely bring himself to look at the man he held responsible for his nephew's death.

"No, thanks," Kevlar said.

"C'mon, I owe you for that wonderful deal we made. I know you made a shit load of money off those steroids. You should be buying me a drink," Angelo said.

In that instance, Kevlar envisioned himself taking his Moet bottle and beating Angelo to death. The thought of standing in a pool of Angelo's blood at his feet made him smile.

"C'mon, it'll be fun. Besides I got a deal for you that will make you more money than you ever made with those steroids."

Kevlar agreed to throw a few back with Angelo. They headed to the club's exclusive area where each guy enjoyed the attention of the sexy women in their vicinity. After two bottles of Dom Pérignon and an intense debate over the Knicks championship drought, Angelo got down to business. He revealed his love for street basketball, which was first introduced to him by AND 1 mix tapes. Skip To My Lou, Headache, Hot Sauce, and Big Escalade were the players that gave him the most joy in the past. More recently, he'd become a huge Young Moolah fan. He grew animated as he spoke about the way Barkley toyed with the competition and made spectacular plays. Once he rattled off the list of highlights he observed and heard about, Angelo began to unveil his scheme. The get-rich-quick scam was a last ditch effort to recoup the enormous amount of cash he lost at a big poker game in Moscow. Instead of paying millionaire scion Alexander Volkoff the five hundred thousand he lost to him, Angelo was able to orchestrate a more lucrative bet that involved the Russian national basketball team. Angelo chuckled to himself wondering how he made it out of Russia that weekend. Throughout most of the high stakes Texas Hold'em game, Angelo infuriated Volkoff with his talk of American street basketball. The initial bet began at one million dollars. Both men tried to make the other blink by escalating the wager. The longer they went back and forth, the less it became less about a bet. The verbal jousting took center stage, with each combatant trying to show the other who had the bigger dick by making threats and bragging about possessions. When they finally stopped talking with their Johnsons and began thinking sensibly, an astounding four million-dollar agreement was secured as the winning prize. This wager was a huge gamble for Volkoff. He was next in line to run a Russian organized crime family, and was always getting himself into situations that made him more of a liability than a beloved son. Much of his troubles were due to his temper, which was exactly the fire that spurred him to make such a bet with Angelo. The thought of wining four million dollars and shutting Angelo up was all the motivation Volkoff needed to agree to the bet. His father was a high-ranking government official with ties to the Russian mob, so bringing the team's best five players to New York was not a problem. The Russian team had just won the gold in the European championships and finished third in the world championships. In Volkoff's mind, the game was between his country's team and a squad of housing project trash. He projected the game would be the easiest four million he's ever made.

There was a very good reason for Volkoff's confidence. He had a basketball giant on his side. Dmitri Kaslov was expected to be the next Russian import to land in the NBA draft. He could jump. He could shoot. He played defense. His handsome features and blue eyes made him catnip for corporations wanting to sell products in Russia. He was definitely going to be a problem for Angelo, however, it wasn't a problem that could not be solved by sliding Dmitri a lucrative offer he couldn't refuse. He was only months away from receiving a wealthy NBA contract, but two hundred grand in cash was just the right number to make Dmitri give Volkoff the finger. Dmitri agreed to throw the game. Once Angelo scheduled a delivery of the cash to Dmitri, he easily had the first component of his plan secure. Now he was pitching Kevlar. He offered Kevlar and his team a quarter of a million dollars to win the game.

The offer was insulting to Kevlar on two fronts. "First off, how the fuck you offering compensation that's only fifty thousand more than you givin' one nigga? Second, my guys don't need a game to be fixed in order for them to take care of business."

Kevlar agreed to make his team the final component in Angelo's plot, but only if their winnings were paid upfront and had a lot more zeroes attached. Reluctantly, Angelo agreed to Kevlar's stipulation and offered up a cool million. Both men celebrated their deal with another bottle of Dom. Angelo was feeling ecstatic about his plan coming together and Kevlar was smiling inside knowing he just planted his seeds of vengeance. And it was only a matter of time before they would bear fruit.

Chapter 10

There was silence after Kevlar completed his story. Barkley and his teammates did not utter a word because they were confused about the task they were asked to execute.

"So do you want us to throw a game that is already being thrown?" Khakalak asked.

"No, I want you to help me kill the motherfucker that took the life of my little nephew. Help me put that bitch in the ground," Kevlar said.

His tone and words paralyzed his team, rendering them mute. No one dared to look at each other or even glance in Kevlar's direction. The room was silent until the person who always said the least spoke up. Man Child's stuttering kept him from feeling comfortable with long conversations. He chose his words wisely and made sure they were heard.

"If we lose this game, who is he coming after us? Because I don't know a whole lotta people that will lose one million dollars and not be looking to make someone pay for it," Man Child said.

All of his fellow team members turned their attention toward Kevlar in anticipation of his answer.

"I love you guys like family. There isn't a situation I would put you in where I could not protect you. We do this right, everybody is richer and nobody is looking over their shoulder. Are you guys in?" Kevlar asked.

The team was silent. Each member pondered what direction was the right way to go on the life-changing opportunity. Khakalak was the first to step up. He agreed to play the game and go through with Kevlar's plan. The twins fell in line behind him. Barkley joined the plot as well. Man Child walked over to Kevlar and looked him the eyes.

"If I do this, will my family be protected?" Man Child asked.

Without hesitation Kevlar guaranteed their safety.

Kevlar's plan was set. He kept Moncrief out of the loop. The less people who knew about his plan for revenge, the better. Besides, Moncrief loved the game so much, anything that involved tainting it would have been a hard pill for him to swallow. Barkley stayed behind to talk with Kevlar after the rest of the team left the lounge. He did not have any questions about what Kevlar had cooked up. His questions revolved who Angelo was. The man Kevlar marked for death was heavy on his mind since being introduced to him. Barkley knew he had seen Angelo somewhere before but could not remember where. He expected his curiosity about Angelo to be cured by Kevlar, but that was an inaccurate assumption. Although Barkley's questions were simple, he was given anything but the answers he was looking for. Kevlar shot down any questions pertaining to the game or Angelo. The more questions Barkley asked, the angrier Kevlar became.

"I know I've seen this guy on television and just wanted to know if he had been arrested on the news or was a regular on some dumb ass reality show," Barkley said.

Kevlar grabbed Barkley by the collar and threw him up against a wall. "Stop with all the fucking questions! The less you know, the more likely you are to live. I'm trying to protect your inquisitive ass. Understand?" Kevlar yelled.

Amid the shocking reaction to his simple questions,

Barkley got Kevlar to release him from his clutches. Barkley left the lounge, baffled by Kevlar's actions. Instead of letting it drop, it increased Barkley's appetite for answers immensely. There were now clouds of suspicion hanging over Kevlar and his scheme to wipe out a man he didn't want to talk about. Barkley wanted information on his boss' mark and he knew just who to ask.

Born was the first person to come to mind. He had always been able to give Barkley any information he needed. It was like he was an underworld website. The two friends hadn't hung out or spoken to each other for months. Barkley initially thought Born left town after their last conversation in Harlem. He later heard his friend was still in town but was keeping a low profile, collecting corner rent from the street pharmacist feeding the addicts. With less than a week before the game, Barkley put out word he was looking for Born. The clock was ticking and Barkley knew he did not have a lot of time, so his investigation did not stop at the street level.

Next up was Detective Shamus Harrison. Although they had not seen each other since the incident with the gun inside Harrison's car, Barkley knew he could get a straight shot of truth without the chaser from his him. It had almost been a year since the two of them parted ways that afternoon in Brooklyn, and the suicidal thoughts that surfaced during their last meeting were the farthest they had ever been from Barkley's mind.

The New York street basketball circuit had become his oyster. He now looked up to Kevlar as his savior and sort of a father figure. Since joining the team, there hadn't been any reason for Barkley to question the fatherly advice he'd received, but when Kevlar shut down the open dialogue they'd always had between them, a rash of speculation began to spread. Some unexpected turns had also surfaced in the life of Barkley's old friend. Things were looking up for Harrison as well. A few major drug busts put him on the fast track to superstardom in the police department. His major investigations resulted in the capture and conviction of major players on a regular basis. There were some suspicions about his methods of obtaining information, as well as whispers about missing funds that were obtained during drug bust. The "toys" Harrison would parade in front of his colleagues fueled these suspicions. He cruised the city in a brand new Lexus, donned designer duds, and called a newly rehabilitated Harlem brownstone home sweet home. In the minds of many of his fellow blue brethren, Harrison had gotten his hands dirty more than a few times. A cop with an ex-wife, and alimony coupled with child support and so many expensive possessions would have definitely landed on the radar of Internal Affairs, but since he did his job—closed cases and got the worst of the worst off the street—it kept him safely away from being investigated. Plus, Harrison had a few rabbis within the force who made sure his shit didn't stink to the point where the stench could be smelled outside of the stationhouse.

Barkley did not have any contact information on Harrison. There was never any need to have it. Barkley appreciated all the help Harrison gave him over the years, but palling around with a cop was not a smart move in the streets of Bed-Stuy or nearby Crown Heights. He wondered how he could get a message to him until he remembered seeing Harrison's former partner moonlighting as a security guard at Harlem Lanes. Barkley hopped in a cab to make the long trek from Brooklyn to Harlem in hopes of getting Harrison's contact information. On his way uptown, he began to think his fishing expedition was a waste of time. Kevlar's refusal to answer a simple question was definitely the driving force behind Barkley's curiosity, but he wondered if he was making a mountain out of a mole hill. Just as he was about to make the decision to call off his own investigation, the cab pulled up in front of Harlem Lanes. He almost instructed the cabbie to take him back to Brooklyn, but Barkley spotted Harrison talking to his old partner inside the lobby area of the bowling alley. He paid the thirty-five-dollar fare and exited the cab thinking of what he would say. Barkley decided to take what he thought was a humorous approach to reintroduce himself to his former guardian angel.

"Can I borrow your burner? I need to blow my fucking brains out."

Harrison turned around with a menacing look only to see it was the young kid he had grown to love and care about over many years. The surprise reunion induced an immediate reaction. He put Barkley in a playful headlock "You little shit! Where the fuck you been keeping yourself? I ain't heard nothing from you since that day you was talking crazy. Now you show up outta the blue. Man, we gotta catch up," Harrison said. They headed up the street to the Moonstar Diner to chat about what had been going on in their respective lives.

"Oh! So you're Young Moolah. The streets have turned you into some type of Stephon Marbury/Allen Iverson/Kyrie Irving hybrid. Keep it up. Somebody's gonna come knocking on your door. Just be wary of Kevlar. That guy has kept his nose clean for the past few months, but he was into a lot of shit back in the day. So watch your back with him," Harrison said.

"That's what I wanted to talk to you about," Barkley said and proceeded to tell Harrison about the game with the Russians, leaving out the team's plan to throw it. He did not feel like hearing a lecture and did not want to discuss morals and gamesmanship when he knew all he cared about was getting information on Angelo. He told Harrison he knew he saw Angelo somewhere else before, but couldn't recall where. Harrison responded to Barkley's inquiry by telling him the name Angelo didn't ring any bells, but he assured Barkley he would do what he could to find out more information. With only a day and a half before the game, time was running out. The brief reunion ended with both agreeing to meet up on the day of the game an hour before tip-off.

As Harrison watched Barkley hop in a cab and head off, he had a bad feeling about the upcoming game. He picked up his phone and began his own investigation.

"Yeah, it's me. Tell Johnny Bats I need a sit down with him ASAP. It's about that little shit, Angelo. I need some answers before I put down on a game," Harrison said.

Chapter 11

It was the day of the game and Harrison had no answers for Barkley. His request for a sit down meeting with Johnny Bats fell on deaf ears. Harrison knew where to find him, but given the nature of their relationship, just showing up would surely result in a starring role in one the FBI's surveillance videos.

Johnny Bats, whose real name was Johnny Alturo, began his organized crime career as mafia muscle, but then used less violent skills to move up the Capilini family business ladder. He had a movie star look and lots of fans; the feds were definitely one of his biggest. His charisma was legendary. Stories ranged from him charming a schoolteacher into changing a grade for his son, to him fucking the desperate housewife of the federal agent who spent countless hours watching him. No one had a clue that Harrison was joined at the hip to one of the most dangerous organized crime families in the tri-state area.

Harrison had become one of the most trusted contractors in the Capilini family. Whatever the Northern New Jersey crime family called on him to do, he made it look clean, and like it was official police business.

Two hours before the game started, Harrison got a call telling him where he could meet Johnny Bats. The location was just over an hour drive from New York City to Central New Jersey. There was no way he was going to make that trip and make his scheduled pre-game meeting with Barkley. He decided to go to the meeting with Johnny Bats and place a phone call to Barkley to give him the information he discovered.

Harrison arrived at an apartment building in Trenton an hour and a half after leaving his Brooklyn station house. He was wary about going in. He had never met Johnny Bats at this location. Thoughts of getting whacked entered his mind so he walked cautiously, but confidently, his hand in easy reach of his side arm. After three knocks on the front door of an apartment, a woman dressed in a silk robe answered the door. She welcomed him into the apartment and pointed toward the bedroom.

"Johnny, you back there? Hey, Johnny!" Harrison yelled.

The toilet flushed and Johnny emerged from the bedroom without washing his hands. He walked over and embraced Harrison.

"I'm sorry for taking so long to get back in touch with you. With the feds up my ass I gotta be careful about where I meet up with folks. But you know this already," Johnny said.

"Yeah I know. So I'll make this brief. I put down some heavy cash on a game and next thing I hear Angelo has his hands all in it. I got my money on this squad of street ballers, but you never know what to expect with these kids," Harrison said.

"It's the best bet you ever made," .

With excitement in his voice, Johnny Bats laid out the plans the Capilini family had set in motion. He began with the story behind Angelo and his relationship with his father, Vincent Capilini, the head of the family. Angelo would piss plenty of people off in the illegal gambling world, but no one knew why he was seemingly untouchable. Born to a Russian mother and Italian father,

Angelo was able to navigate both worlds. He never received the attention he wanted from his father. Vincent acknowledged his paternal connection to his youngest son, but only to a small group of people and never in public, except for on one occasion. After his last acquittal on racketeering charges, photographers captured the father and son embracing outside a Newark, New Jersey federal courthouse. Out of all the family members he hugged that day, a photo of him and Angelo was what ran on the front pages of New York City and New Jersey newspapers.

Tired of being the son who was secretly sired, Angelo came up with a plan to gain the love and acceptance he always wanted. He set up a game-changing move that would give his father's family a seat at the big table with New York City's crime families. Located so close to New York City, the Capilini clan always had Big Apple aspirations. Taking from the downtrodden and the druggies was no problem; the difficult task of setting up shop and invading New York City neighborhoods was the migraine the Capilinis couldn't shake.

The first phase of the New York City invasion was the bet made between Angelo and Alexander Volkoff. His love for his country made him an easy mark. He had gotten into debates over less when it came to defending Russia. Comparing American street basketball to the Russian national team combined with a shit load of money was just the right kind of bait to get Volkoff to bite. The second phase called for the players in the game to do everything they were instructed to do. That meant Bk To Tha Fullest needed to win.

"You put a major coup like this on the shoulders of some street ballers; the old man signed off on this?"

Harrison asked.

"Are you fucking stupid? You think we've waited this long to make a move and have it controlled by some jumping jungle bunnies?" Johnny asked.

"So who or what is the insurance policy?"

The duffel bag full of cash dropped off at Dmitri Kaslov's New York City hotel room was the guarantee Johnny Bats was speaking of. Angelo assured the rest of the family, paying off the Russian team's star player and giving Kevlar and his team enough incentive to win the game would pave the way for their power move in New York.

"And if this Dmitri guy stiffs you guys, what happens then?" Harrison asked.

"All of that has been addressed," Johnny said.

Angelo made sure Dmitri knew if his team was on the winning end of the game, his five-year-old son's genitals would wind up on a key chain. The Capilini family was poised for a major win, and that win meant acquiring the luxuries and privileges connected to having a high-ranking member of the Russian mob by the balls.

"You're talking warfare. You think the Russian mob is gonna bend over and let you give it to them up the ass? There's gonna be rivers of blood running through Brooklyn and Newark," Harrison said.

"My friend, my friend, you just continue to show me in so many ways you don't know shit. Let me finish before you show how fucking stupid you are," Johnny said.

The plan was to use the four million dollars owed by Alexander Volkoff as a bargaining chip. The last thing Nikolai Volkoff would want is for news of his son's multi-million-dollar debt to get out in the streets. Ratting out the competition was not in the plans, but there would be a high price tag attached to keeping quiet. With a smug look on his face, Johnny Bats described how the family was going to make its introduction into New York City's underworld. The takeover would begin with taking a slice of prostitution and sex trafficking. They would then gradually take over their drug trafficking sector by controlling all transportation of product into New York.

Harrison's phone rang, interrupting Johnny Bats, but he ignored the call. He knew who was trying to reach him. It was a half hour past the time he agreed to meet Barkley. Seconds later, his phone rang again. Sensing Johnny Bats' aggravation, Harrison put his phone on vibrate to avoid additional interruptions.

"That was a good move. You know how I hate to be interrupted." Continuing, Johnny Bats informed Harrison that he is the final component. The family was going to need some muscle to make sure execution of the plan stayed on course.

"Am I being asked or am I being told?"

Johnny Bats erupted into laughter. He explained to Harrison at this point in the game combined with all that he has done for the family, there is no debate or dialogue about what he will or will not do. His orders for Harrison were simple in his mind—form a team of cops to be judge, jury, and executioner if any of the Russians got out of line. He was also ordered to create diversions if anyone got any ideas about taking a look into the new way things were going to be done. Harrison quickly began to realize he was sinking himself deep into a life there was no way out of. The dirt he previously did could easily be washed away.

What he was now being asked to do was the kind work where the dirt gets under your fingernails. Washing it away would take a lot more cleansing. This was completely different—and much grimier.

"How much time do I have to put together a team?" Harrison asked.

Johnny Bats gave him one week. After the game, Alexander Volkoff was going to be abducted to make sure his father would play nice. Once he agreed to the Capilini's terms, the transition of power was going to start immediately. The Capilini family knew regime change would not come peacefully on all fronts. They expected to drop a few bodies, but it would merely be looked at as a cost of doing business. Johnny Bats looked at his platinum diamond encrusted watch and noticed the time for tip off was just minutes away. His excitement oozed from his pores. He called for his girlfriend to pop a bottle of bubbly he had in her refrigerator to toast the start of a new relationship with Harrison and the beginning of a new era for the Capilini family.

When Harrison finally left the apartment, he felt empty. In his mind, each step he took towards the elevator was a step he was taking toward the death chamber. He knew he was embarking on what was equivalent to a suicide mission. Regardless of what plan the Capilini family had in place, the Russian mob was never going to agree to the terms being shoved up their asses. There was going to be blood spilled. And keeping the splatter from peppering him was going to be damn near impossible. Thoughts of committing unthinkable crimes and dancing with the devil created a bout with nausea within Harrison. He managed to make it to his car before the contents inside his stomach erupted from his mouth. Hunched over next to his car, vomit showered the pavement. After spewing out all he had consumed over the previous two hours, Harrison noticed he had dropped his phone nearby. His BlackBerry cell phone lit up. Harrison wondered if it was his first order from the family. Was he going have to kill someone? Was he going to have to take care of the abduction himself? A number of thoughts ran through his mind. He picked up the phone and wiped the bit of vomit that had managed to land on it. He slowly put the phone to his ear, and waited for the worst.

"You have one new message. Message was received at 5:45 p.m. This is Bark, my nig. Where the fuck were you, man. I waited for you at the meeting spot for as long as I could. I expect niggas to be the late ones. White boys like you are always on time. You probably had some police situation you had to handle, but no biggie. It's water under the bridge and the information I wanted isn't going to help me much anyway. There is a lot more going on than I revealed to you the other day. I wanted to know about Angelo, because even though he is financing the game and paying us a shit load of money to win this game, my teammates and I have been told to the throw the game. I'm kinda bummed about it because I wanted to see if we could beat them. I also hear they got this nasty dude who is supposed to go pro next year, so I wanted to see where my game was compared to his. The crazy thing about that shit is, Angelo is paying the dude off, so he plays shitty. Kinda funny 'cuz Kevlar's got this vendetta against Angelo, and he has no clue what Kevlar's got cooking up for his ass. Shit as long as I get paid, I'm good. And I know Kevlar wouldn't put us in some crazy situation where it's

dangerous for us to do this. I kinda wish I told you about our plans; you could've won yourself some extra dough. If anything, you may wanna come down to the game. Shit is gonna hit the fan I'm sure of it. According to Kevlar, this dude stands to lose like three hundred grand. If you wanna come out the game is at Gaucho's Gym in the Bronx. They only letting a select few people in, but if you flash your badge you shouldn't have any problem getting through the doors. Holla. *To delete this message press seven. For more options press...*"

Harrison hung up the phone in disbelief. Initially he felt an enormous amount of weight lifted from his shoulders. The mental anguish brought on by anxiety started to subside. He chuckled at the notion of the collapse that was about to blindside the Capilini family. His laughter quickly evolved into an all-out celebration. The exhilaration manifested into giant smile across Harrison's face. Cheesing from ear to ear, Harrison got in his car as if he'd been granted a stay of execution. He cued up Frank Sinatra's "Luck Be A Lady" on his iPod, thinking Old Blue Eyes would hit him in the right spot. The song blared from his car speakers and interrupted all thoughts except for one; the vendetta Kevlar had against Angelo stuck in his head. From there his brain went on tangents. He thought if there was a vendetta that meant there was a prior conflict. The cop's brain began churning out several scenarios. He thought, *If Kevlar was carrying a vendetta off some shit that happened in the past, he's gotta have a deep hatred for Angelo that was deep enough to motivate murder.* Harrison pulled over to the service lane on the New Jersey Turnpike to piece together the puzzle inside his head. Just as cars raced passed his parked vehicle, thoughts were racing through his mind as he pondered what scheme Kevlar could possibly be attempting to hatch. He then began to think about repercussions. The Capilini family was putting a lot of money behind this power move on the Russians. Failure to execute was not an option. And if that happened, someone was going to pay with their lives. Harrison knew Vincent Capilini wasn't going to kill his own son. *So who after that? The team,* he thought. Regardless if it could be proven or not, the Capilini family was going to need to save face and taking out a team of street ballers would allow them to do that and send a message. If the team had a target on them, that also meant Barkley did as well. A quick look at his watch and Harrison knew he was too late and too far to keep his friend from playing. But he could get to him before the game was over and get him out of there before the mayhem occurred. He buckled up and mashed the pedal to the floor. Just as Harrison sped off, the officials at the scorer's table inside Gaucho's Gym hit the buzzer for the game to start. The raucous crowd cheered loudly as both teams approached center court. The teams were in position for tip-off. The referee blew his whistle, and up went the ball.

Chapter 12

There was no pre-game pageantry. No announcement of players. The game between BK To Tha Fullest and the Russian national team was a battle of establishment versus raw talent. It featured the city's best team against a group of players who earned their stripes playing against the best in the world. Both teams had their cheering sections, the loudest being the two spectators with the most to lose, Angelo Capilini and Alexander Volkoff. After winning the tip-off, the majority of the small crowd displayed their allegiance to Barkley and his teammates. The sideline opposite of the team's benches was standing room only. The audience of high rollers, criminals, and killers stood adjacent to each other. Each spectator had their own reason for cheering for the respective teams, which was likely love of country or love of money. The Capilini family and the Russian mob were well represented, and kept their space from one another.

From the start of the game, both teams kept up a NASCAR-like pace, playing fast and furious. Whether a shot was made or missed, each team sprinted to the opposite end of the court to score. The breakneck pace of the game kept the spectators on edge. Although six out of the ten players on the court knew a pre-determined outcome was in place, both teams were putting on a performance that led most in the crowd to believe the game was up for grabs. Barkley and his teammates knew the game plan was to keep it close, but their competitive spirit produced a bit of bravado. They knew the Russian team

91

was playing with a handicap, but so were they. And they could not help but think they were just as good and talented as their European adversaries. Midway through the first half, players on BK To Tha Fullest started trash talking with the competition. The Russians were not very fluent in English. However, they could understand what it meant when Double-Double started calling their team weak bitches. Although he did not say anything, Khakalak received the repercussions of his teammates taunting. He was in the paint preparing to rise for a rebound when a Russian elbow to his midsection canceled his lift off. He fell to the ground in agony, sparking a shoving match between the teams. The game took on a different tone after that incident. The small melee even got Dmitri Kaslov's juices flowing and he decided to showcase his NBA potential. He hit four consecutive three pointers, sparking a rout that produced fifteen unanswered point by the Russians. The street ballers had just experienced an unstoppable force like they had never seen. A quick timeout gave them a chance to catch their breath and get an earful from Moncrief. His words were not kind, but they were constructive.

"I can't believe what I'm fucking seeing out there. You letting Drago do whatever the fuck he wants to do out there. This is your city. This is your house. And you're playing like somebody is just going to give you something," Moncrief said.

The hard-edged coach spoke the truth, but he had no idea how truthful his words were. Barkley and his teammates were putting on a show, but not the kind their coach had become accustomed to seeing. His love of the game could be seen in his eyes and felt from his voice.

Moncrief spent the entire thirty-second timeout delivering a fiery speech. His team could only lower their heads in secret shame. They knew what a win would do for Moncrief and deep inside each of their hearts, there was an urge to give it to him. But that meant crossing Kevlar, and that was something that could not be done if they wanted to continue breathing. Moncrief continued his rant until the buzzer went off to signify the end of the timeout. He was so disgusted with the team he told them to get the fuck off his bench and not to comeback unless they were ready to play the way he knew they could. With their heads staring at the ground, the team returned to the court. Before the start of play, Khakalak called another timeout and gathered his teammates for an impromptu player only team meeting.

"We all know what this is. And we all know what we 'pose to do. But just because we were told to lay down don't mean we gotta take it in the ass. C'mon, y'all, let's give that old grumpy nigga over there something to cheer about," said Khakalak. After hearing Khakalak's inspirational words, each member began to raise his head in agreement. They all put a hand on top of one another's and shouted their signature war chant, "Ahhh shit!!!"

They walked onto the court with the street ball swagger that made them a formidable team in anyone's backyard. With five minutes left in the half and seventeen points behind, BK To Tha Fullest was ready to make some noise. Khakalak got things started with a three-pointer that went straight through the net without touching an alloy of the iron rim. Barkley kept the momentum going with the wizardry of his ball handling skills. He was the puppeteer and the ball was his puppet. The Russians were kept off balance with cross over dribbles and speed. Barkley was getting past his Russian defenders with ease, making more than a few of them hit the hardwood with their backsides. The court was his canvas and he was drawing up plays for each of his teammates, dishing the ball to them play after play. A dunk here. A three-pointer there. It all began to add up, evaporating the Russians lead and putting them in the lead by five points with twenty seconds to go in the half.

On the defensive end, Dmitri was placed in a vacuum. The team suffocated him each time the Russians got the ball. Unable to get the ball to their star player, the Russians offense quickly began to hyperventilate and BK To Tha Fullest was not giving any breathing room.

The buzzer sounded to end the half, leaving the Russians without a basket for the last five minutes of the first half. Alexander Volkoff was livid as the teams walked into the locker rooms. The Russians gave him a glimpse of victory in the beginning stages of the game, but their play in the latter portion of the first half made him panic. He was now worried about the multi-million-dollar price tag that would hang over his head if the Russians were to lose. He did not hide his anxiety. The walls of the Russian team's locker room did little to lower the volume of Volkoff's tantrum. He spoke loudly and he made threats—the kind of threats that hit home. Each of the Russian players knew who they were dealing with and how far of a reach he had. They were not in danger, but their families could be. Like a tornado, his tirade hopped from one player to another. Ironically, the player charged with the task of throwing the game for the other side received the least amount of threats and tongue-lashing. Maybe it was the barrage of points he put up just before half time. Perhaps his play gave the Russians the best chance to win, and Volkoff did not want to rattle his star player. His peaceful and constructive approach toward Dmitri didn't last long. He kicked everyone on the team out of the locker room except for his star player. After the Russian players left, two muscular Russian mobsters entered. Dmitri started to get nervous when one of the men locked the door. Alexander calmly sat next to Dmitri before instructing him to open the locker he was sitting in front of. When he refused, the two mobsters grabbed and forced him to do what he had been instructed. Once Dmitri opened the locker, he knew his life was in danger. The duffle bag full of cash he'd received hours before the game was now directly in front of his face. Death was hovering above his head and he wondered if he was taking his last breaths. Volkoff had several reasons to end Dmitri's life right at that moment, but he had millions of reasons to keep him alive. No one could guard Dmitri when he really played. Now that his life was on the line, Volkoff was sure he'd be unstoppable in the second half of the game. He had to be; his life depended on it.

The scene across the hall was more festive. Moncrief couldn't have been happier with the way his troops fought back on the court to put themselves in a position to win the game. Angelo was even happier. With his arms draped around two husky enforcers who looked like they had done a three to five stint in Sing Sing, Angelo swung through the locker room doors shouting words of praise and adulation. Unbeknownst to him, his applause was for a team that was twenty minutes away from turning his life upside down, and setting up the Capilini family for annihilation. Because of their performance on the court, Barkley and his teammates were able to disguise their true marching orders. Angelo could see a win within his grasp, which in his mind, equated to family acceptance and a father's love. He hugged every single player before he left, even managing to sneak one in on Kevlar. That moment of affection made all the players raise their heads in astonishment. Following Angelo's exit from the locker room, Moncrief drilled the team with inspirational words. Kevlar stood in the corner of the locker room and could only smile as he thought of his puppet mastery. His plan was coming together and he knew it was only a matter of time before he was going to see the demise of Angelo.

Gridlocked traffic on the New Jersey Turnpike stalled Harrison's efforts to reach Barkley. The delays were maddening. Rush hour commuters flooded the roadways every day during the same hours. Unfortunately for Harrison, that was when he embarked on his journey to save Barkley, and the preliminary stages of road rage were setting in. Instead of speeding toward his destination, his vehicle crawled at a snail-like pace as he tried to get to the Bronx. The New Jersey Turnpike was no longer the fastest way for Harrison to get to the Bronx. He was also getting more upset with the fact that he was never going to make it in time to stop Kevlar's plan. Mental exhaustion set in as he tried to think of alternative routes to take. Finally, a breakthrough. Posted right in clear view was a sign for the Staten Island and the Outer Bridge Crossing, which was a better route than the snarled traffic Harrison was driving in. . Taking that exit off the turnpike would definitely put him back in New York City, but at its most southern point. It was not the option Harrison was looking for since he was trying to get to the most northern borough in the city, but he had no other choice. Traffic had come to standstill and Barkley's life was in jeopardy, so that was his only option.

Now that he had selected his alternative route, getting there was going to be just as much of a headache as figuring out his next move. Starting from the left lane, getting to the right lane to exit was not going to be an easy task. New Jersey turnpike drivers were rarely cordial to fellow drivers, especially during episodes of gridlock. As traffic began to creep forward, Harrison began to make his move, honking his horn and pointing his finger toward the exit to signify the direction he was going. The frustrated drivers ignored his plea for a lane change. His attempts to be aggressive were met with near accidents and verbal expletives. Harrison's passive-aggressive approach was not working, so he elected to use more of an authoritative approach.

"Hey, I need to get over. I'm on police business," said Harrison as he raised his badge for the Latino couple to see. The Latino motorist lowered his salsa tunes and told his wife and two kids to lower their voices to better hear the adjacent white man barking his request. "I need to get over. I'm on New York Police Department business. It's an emergency," Harrison said with his badge raised in eye's view.

Before he could utter another word, Harrison received the answer to his request in the form of a raised middle finger and a voice with a heavy Hispanic accent that said, "This is Jersey, bitch."

That was the final straw. Harrison reached his boiling point and in one motion tossed his badge onto the passenger side front seat and pulled his gun from his holster. "Now can I get over?!" yelled Harrison.
Without hesitation, drivers in the adjacent lanes obliged the request of the pistol-packing motorist. He waved his gun

until he finally made it to the exit. He took the ramp and sped off, hoping his new route would get him to the Bronx in time.

Chapter 13

BZZZZ! The buzzer sounded, signifying the start of the second half. The teams began the back end of the game just how they started the first half: a barrage of offense with pockets of defense. There were defensive stops here and there, but those were few and far in between. Both teams seemed to be scoring at will. If the Russian team dropped a three, BK To Tha Fullest responded right away with their own three-pointer. It was a heavyweight title fight and neither side was pulling punches. Although Barkley and his teammates were prepared to drastically decrease the intensity of their play, the competitive fire kept them juiced longer than they anticipated. The team was feeling good about taking it to the Russians. They were executing the beat down of a global basketball powerhouse, and doing it by playing their style of ball. The Russians were wounded prey, but they were fighting as if their lives depended on it. For some, the game did represent a life or death situation. They dove for loose balls. Under the radar of the referees, they used every dirty tactic they could think of. As long as it led to a basket, they did not care.

With just under two minutes remaining, Moncrief called timeout. His team was leading by four points and he wanted them to recognize the situation. Moncrief couldn't hide his excitement. He was elated by the possible turn of events. His team was about to get a major win that would be talked about for years to come. He instructed them to be ready for any defensive schemes thrown their way. His message would have been inspiring to Barkley and his teammates in most situations, but it didn't matter that day.

The timeout was spent diagramming a play to get the ball in bounds. As he shouted instructions, Kevlar walked behind the bench so each member of his team could see him. There was no need for a nod or any gestures. The look in Kevlar's eyes said it all. The message was clear: keep the plan in place and lose the game. Before leaving the bench, Kevlar pulled Man Child in an embrace and gave him a message.

"You know what to do if things get too close. I'm counting on you. And if you gotta do what we talked about, that paper gets a lot bigger for you. I'll take care of you," Kevlar said.

Man Child turned to walk onto the court stone faced. He'd been given his orders and if the scenario he and Kevlar discussed were to play out, his mission was simple. Man Child was going to play the goat if the team got too close to winning the game. If it meant throwing the ball out of bounds or fouling an opposing player, he was going to do whatever he had to do to turn the ball over to the Russians. Combined with the extra money he stood to make from Kevlar, refusing to play the role of the team klutz was not an option at that point.

Just as the referee blew the whistle for play to begin, Harrison came running through the entrance to the gym startling some of the spectators. The armed security officers initially stopped him from walking toward the court, but Angelo cleared his pass before things got rough. He called him over, smiling as he motioned for him to walk in his direction. The score was definitely the source behind Angelo's wide smile and happiness. Unfortunately for him, his grin would shortly be erased. An episode of events was about to take place that would replace his joy with rage. The referee blew the whistle for the game to begin. He handed the ball to Khakalak and started the five-second count allotted for in-bounding the ball. The Russian defense was impregnable. Any passing lane that appeared to be open was closed within fractions of a second. Five seconds had expired. The referee blew the whistle.

"Five-second violation! Russian ball!"

The Russian spectators erupted into an ecstatic frenzy. They celebrated as if they had won the Cold War. With each team out of timeouts, both coaches shouted instructions over the volume of the raucous crowd. For the Russian team, the game plan was simple. Get the ball to Dmitri and get the fuck out of the way. Given the threat of a painful demise hanging over his head, giving Dmitri the keys to drive his team to victory was the best play for the Russians to call. They were able to inbound the ball with no problem. BK To Tha Fullest mounted a man-on-man defensive press. Khakalak was given the assignment of stopping Dmitri. It was a task he had not come close to mastering throughout the second half of the game. Thirty seconds remained in the game. Dmitri was looking for his shot, but could not shake Khakalak. His speed and endurance made him a formidable foe during the waning seconds of the game. The Russian superstar made a quick dash to right side of the key and was forced to pick up his dribble. Khakalak had him trapped. He wasn't going anywhere but up for a shot. A small head fake got Dmitri enough space to draw contact from Khakalak's outstretched arm and get a shot up. It took what seemed like a lifetime for the ball to come down, and when it did, swish! Dmitri scored a three-pointer, pulling his team within one point with just two seconds left. On top of that, he was fouled.

At that moment it seemed like the entire gymnasium was filled with a pro-Russian crowd. The crowd went wild over the spectacular shot. Applause and howls could be heard well outside the walls of the gymnasium. A small group of Russian mobsters were so elated they began to sing the Russian national anthem. The members of the Russian team were also elated they rushed over to embrace their teammate for his late game heroics; hugging him so hard the entire group fell to the floor. Following a few seconds of celebration, the team rose to their feet smiling ear to ear. All of them were overrun with emotion except for Dmitri. His lack of emotion and blank stare was likely viewed as an attempt to maintain concentration on the foul shot he was about to take. With the game on the line and under the circumstances at hand, the men with the most currency to lose, both felt victory was within reach. In Angelo's mind, he'd paid good money for Dmitri to miss the foul shot. In Volkoff's mind, the threat he made to kill Dmitri and his entire family was enough to guarantee he made the shot.

Throughout the Russian superstar's career he'd built his reputation on coming through in the clutch. On this day, he was ready to shed that image for a big payday and let his team down. However, he couldn't let his family down. They weren't going to die because of his greed. He locked eyes with Angelo as he walked to the stripe to shoot his foul shot. Angelo did not nod nor did he make any gestures toward him. There was enough time left in the game to make something happen off of a rebound, but in Angelo's mind the game was over. All he needed was a missed shot from Dmitri and someone from BK To Tha Fullest to get the rebound. While Dmitri was practicing his shooting form and envisioning himself making the shot, there was a another pawn in this game being moved into position. Kevlar locked eyes with Man Child and made a gesture with his hand. The wide-bodied center acknowledged the signal and began to execute the emergency plan to ensure a Russian win. He began to forcefully nudge his Russian counterpart with an elbow to jockey for position in case of a rebound. The referee observed the dirty tactics and issued a warning, hoping that would be enough to bring a halt to any ugly play in the final seconds of the game.

"Number fifty-five, one more move like that and I'm gonna send a tech your way," the referee said.

Referees never liked to have a role in deciding the outcome of a close, but the threat of calling a technical foul was real and delivered in a stern manner. Once the threat was delivered, that did nothing to detour the plan Man Child had in his head. He was going to carry out his orders as instructed by Kevlar. After blowing his whistle, the referee handed the ball to Dmitri for his foul shot. He dribbled twice before shooting. Members of both teams rushed to get position for a rebound. Before the ball could hit the rim Man Child swung his elbow upward, connecting with the nose of the Russian player next to him. The blow sent him to the ground as sprinkles of blood splattered the hardwood floor. The shot hit the back of the rim before bouncing high and landing in the arms of Barkley. Shocked by his miss, Dmitri rushed toward Barkley to rip the ball away. The buzzer sounded. Time had expired and from the looks of the scoreboard, BK To Tha Fullest had won the game. Angelo ran toward Moncrief and jumped into his arms. Before the pair could share their celebratory embrace with the rest of the team, whistles were blown by both referees as they attempted to regain order on the court. The sound of the whistles silenced the entire gymnasium.

"Foul on number fifty-five for an elbow to the face. Technical foul on number fifty-five for un-sportsmanlike conduct," the referee said.

Angelo was livid. He pushed himself out of Moncrief's arms and ran directly toward the referee who made the call. His anger was evident. He grew angrier by the second. He had just secured the biggest win in his family's history, and it was being stripped away from him. His rage grew and grew. Angelo verbally tore into the referee, using every profane word he could think of, and when he saw it was not affecting the referee in any way, he resorted to more of a violent approach. Angelo pulled his nickel-plated nine-millimeter from his back holster and began to pistol whip the referee. He stood over the referee in attack mode, swiping at him with relentless aggression. Volkoff watched this ordeal unfold before his eyes and quickly grew tired of his adversary's antics. He sent two of his men to pull Angelo off of the referee. The two men made it to within ten steps of Angelo before three of Angelo's men drew their guns and rushed toward the Russian duo heading in the direction of their boss. Feeling threatened as they stared down the barrels of the trio's firearms, the Russians pulled their guns and were quickly backed up by ten other men with firepower of their own. The rest of the Capilini family responded with their own reinforcements and artillery. Both sides had guns drawn, hurling threats in English and Russian. Sensing the possibility of a catastrophic episode with each passing second, Harrison reluctantly put himself in the middle of the firing zone. He knew it was best for cooler heads to prevail and he had the perfect resolution to chill the room. No one in the gym could deny there was a foul committed. The small pool of blood underneath the basket was enough evidence for everyone to agree that there was some harm done under the hoop during Dmitri's foul shot. With a bit of hesitation, Harrison suggest the technical foul be taken away, but let the foul stand. This meant the Russian team would get two shots instead of three. Two made shots was enough to win the game, but making them was definitely going to be the hard part. With a pan from left to right, Volkoff took inventory of the amount of fire power pointed in his direction. Angelo did the same. Even if they made it out alive, there would be hell to pay for any additional heat brought to their families' doorsteps. And with the amount of lives in the cross hairs of men with big guns, the body count alone would have brought on heat neither family could withstand. With the use of a few expletives to get his point across, Angelo ordered his goon squad to lower their guns. Volkoff did the same seconds later. Harrison's diplomatic resolution was accepted and the game was to be decided on the court.

Zydrunas Bure was a rebounding machine for the Russian national team. That was all the 6'9" power forward was ever asked to do for his team and he did it well. Putting the ball in the basket was usually a daunting task for Bure. Doing it with a broken nose from the free throw line was going to make it damn near impossible. Shooting from the charity stripe, would be the only time and place on the court where Zydrunas could shoot free of defenders. But in this current situation, there was a three-headed monster staring him down. To his left, a pistol packing frenzied crowd shouted jeers and insults to fuck with his concentration and make him think about anything but making the two shots. In the middle, a ten foot high basket fifteen feet away. To his right, his teammates, and the heir to a ruthless crime family that could make him and anyone he loved disappear in a very painful way. As he walked to the free throw line, Zydrunas locked his eyes on the rim, not even for a moment taking a glance to his left or his right. He even refused to look at the referee's extended hand with the ball. His peripheral vision provided him with the location of the ball as he reached for it. He took two dribbles and a deep breath and launched his first shot. The ball hit the center of the painted square on the backboard and went right through the rim. That was one. Game tied. His teammates were ecstatic and nearly leapt from their prayer position. They stopped short because they knew Zydrunas had one more shot. Sensing he could possibly lose the game, Angelo ordered two of his men with to go outside to the parking lot and wait for a call from him.

"In ten seconds I'm gonna give you a call. When your phone rings I want you to fire every fucking shell you got in your clip," Angelo said.

Looking a bit dumbfounded and unsure, one of the men asked, "At who?"

Angelo had him lean over so he could whisper the answer in his ear. "In the air you fucking imbecile. What the fuck are you still here for? Go! Go! Wait, wait, give me your phone."

Angelo did not want any attachment to the diversion he was about to execute. His plan was to have his men fire shots just as Zydrunas was taking his final shot. His pre-shot ritual of two dribbles and a deep breath made it easy to time out his shot. Even after making his first shot, Zydrunas' eyes never left the rim. He was focused on the task at hand, and he was not going to let the volume or vulgarity of the crowd deter him from his goal. As he took the ball from the referee, Angelo prepared to hit the call button on the phone to begin his plan. He watched Zydrunas take his first dribble. Just as he took his second, Angelo looked at the phone so he could watch the phone call go through. He erupted into a hysterical tirade, when he saw the phone handed to him had no battery power and immediately shut off after flashing a call failure signal.

Zydrunas took his deep breath and released his shot. The ball rattled in the rim before it shot upward and then back down through the net. His teammates rushed toward the winning shot taker and tackled him on to the court. All of them shed tears as they celebrated their win in spectacular fashion. Volkoff also joined in the celebration. He jumped on the pile of players as if he'd played a role in winning the game. The Russian constituency in the stands was also celebrating. One Russian team supporter pulled a small Russian flag from his inside pocket. He was soon followed by other men who held their country's flag close to their heart in the inside pocket of their jacket.

The celebration was just starting inside, but it was about to come to an abrupt and terrifying end. There was still a two-man firing squad outside waiting for Angelo's call. The ten-second deadline had passed, leaving the two men wondering what to do and forcing them to think. This was a decision way above their pay grade. They argued about firing their guns even though they had not heard from Angelo. The two men each had valid arguments, but arguing with their arms flailing and one hand on a gun with a hairpin trigger, something bad was bound to happen. As the argument reached a fever pitch, an accidental shot was fired. The unintended target was only a windshield. Unfortunately for them it was the windshield of a passing New York City police vehicle. The police van swerved into an adjacent parked car. The officers inside immediately looked in the direction of where they believed the bullet came from. Their assumption about the trajectory of the bullet was confirmed when they saw the guns in the hands of Angelo's goons. The two female officers pulled their guns, and took cover behind a nearby Ford Explorer. They began calling for back up and firing back.

"This is officer Maldonado. 213!213! Shots fired. Officer in need of assistance. Shots fired!" she said.

The exchange of gunfire brought the celebration inside the gym to a startling end. The Russian faction knew the sounds of gunfire were coming from outside, but excitement generated from the win was now erased and replaced with skepticism. It was time for Angelo to pay up and the eruption of gunfire made him look very suspicious. Alexander Volkoff won the bet. He wanted his money, and he wanted it now. He made that very clear with a few expletives to drive home the point.

"Four million in front of me right now. No fucking games."

Angelo had a blank stare on his face since Bure sank his final shot. His bid to finally be accepted by his father had been annihilated. He also had to wrestle with the notion of giving up four million dollars, a large sum of money he did not have. It was also an amount of money that shocked Barkley and his teammates. This was the first time they heard the real wager on the game. They all gave each other a look of shock. No one said anything, but the look on their faces translated into one common thought. *Oh shit, these mafia motherfuckers are gonna kill us for losing this game*, would have been the most fitting. Volkoff continued his rant, growing louder and louder. Tired of being ignored, he pulled a gun from the holster inside of one of his men's jackets. Just as he was about to point it at Angelo, the situation unfolding outside made its way inside the gymnasium. The two men Angelo sent out to the parking lot had returned and they did not have good news.

"There's a shitload of cops out there, and I don't know when but they're definitely coming in. We were having a cigarette and they just starting shooting at us," one of the men said.

Sensing a blood bath was about to occur, Harrison jumped into his mediator role again. "Listen up, I'm a cop. Now that we got that out of the way, those guys are coming in here guns blazing. The best way to get outta here alive and without a case is for you all to give me your guns, lay on the ground, and don't say shit. I mean not a fucking word, except for one. Lawyer. That's all you say. Lawyer."

To keep things peaceful, Volkoff and Angelo agreed to follow Harrison's lead. Them and their men handed over their guns to Harrison as he walked around with a garbage bag. Everyone, including the players, began to lie on the floor. Moments later the SWAT team made their entrance. With guns drawn they told everyone to stay on the ground. It was a peaceful ending, but the stage was also set for an attack on the people responsible for ruining the Capilini's plan to invade New York City.

Chapter 14

The scene inside the police station looked like an assembly line of wise guys and basketball players inside the 153rd precinct. Each person taken into custody was processed and fingerprinted, including Barkley and his teammates. To avoid a full-scale riot inside the precinct, police divided the two factions. The Russian and Italians were placed in two different holding cells. Barkley and all of his teammates, except for Khakalak, were placed with the Russians. Outside of the occasional stare downs, the Russians did not pose any threat. There was nothing for them to really be upset about. Their national team won the game, and they now had the son of a major New Jersey crime boss on the hook for four million dollars.

In the Italian holding pen, things were a bit testier, especially for Khakalak. He played a great game, but in the eyes of Angelo and his crew, he represented failure and the reason for that multi-million-dollar price tag now hanging over the heads of the Capilinis. Khakalak kept to himself and avoided eye contact. He was in survival mode, but his methods of preservation were about to prove to be futile.

"This is why I didn't vote for Barack Obama, 'cause niggers never come through," one of the detained Italians said.

Another chimed in with, "I think we needed some light-skinned niggers; they would've played more like a team, 'cause the dark jungle bunnies can't do shit."

A barrage of racial slurs were hurled at Khakalak. He attempted to move to another area, hoping to see an officer. As he made his move to what he thought was safer ground, someone tripped him, and he landed on his chest. Before he could get up, his face collided with a size ten gator-skinned shoe. In a matter of seconds, Khakalak was pounced on. He was dragged to the back of the cell and pummeled. Blow after the blow came without pause. Until he uttered words that he thought could be his only lifeline.

"It was Kevlar's idea!" Khakalak said.

His words did not mean anything to the crew of ass kickers, but they did arouse the interest of Angelo very quickly. Khakalak suffered a few more blows before Angelo intervened.

"You've got sixty seconds to tell me what you meant," Angelo said.

A mixture of blood and tears streamed down Khakalak's face as he disclosed the details of Kevlar's plot to put Angelo in a body bag. He knew with his confession he was saving his life for the moment, but in the process also signing the death certificates of his teammates. After Khakalak finished his story, Angelo helped him onto his feet. He thanked him for his honesty and told him his words would definitely place him in the good graces of the Capilini family. It was an indirect way to say he could expect to be killed quickly and with little pain. Seconds later, Khakalak was called for by an approaching officer. He was being released with all the other players. There was nothing to hold them on and they were not suspected to be owners of any of the guns confiscated at the gymnasium. As he left, Khakalak turned around to see a smiling Angelo as he was leaving the cell.

"You're my nigga. I got you, don't worry. We'll talk real soon," Angelo said.

Bruised and battered, Khakalak walked out of the police station. His teammates and coach could not utter any words as they watched him walk down the precinct staircase. The reaction to his injuries ranged from disbelief to fear.

"What the fuck happened to you? Who did this to you?" Moncrief said.

"You talked, didn't you? You country bumpkin bitch, you told them everything, didn't you?" Man Child asked.

The concerns and accusations came down on Khakalak ferociously. He was taking a second ass whipping, only this time it was verbal. His teammates' words were coming down as hard as the blows he received inside the holding tank with the Italians. The questions about what he said and what happened became repetitive quickly. Khakalak continuously denied spilling any information, but he was not coming across as believable. Unaware of the ramifications for his players, Moncrief attempted to play buffer between Khakalak and his teammates. His concern was getting his injured player to a hospital. With an authoritative tone, Moncrief called for his players to stand down.

"Back the fuck up, all of you. Something real fishy is goin' on here, but I don't want to know and I don't give a fuck. I'm getting this man to a hospital." Moncrief said.

His words and the inflection he delivered them with was enough to bring the witch-hunt to an end. The team then turned their attention to Kevlar. The mastermind behind the plot had a lot of questions to answer now that the team knew there were targets on their backs. No one knew where he was. Double-Double remembered seeing him being placed in a holding cell that was separate. The team now knew they weren't given all the details, and they wanted him to answer why. Kevlar had more than a few police officers on his payroll, so just before the police raided the gymnasium, he called in a few favors. Thanks to his brigade of dirty cops, he was in and out of the precinct. There was a tidal wave of vengeance coming his way, so he made it his business to vanish. With each passing minute, Barkley and his teammates knew they were losing time to get out of town. Man Child was the first to make an exit. Instead of questioning his dishonest boss, he began focusing on his family. Soon, each player shifted his focus to making a fast getaway. Moncrief and Khakalak hopped into a cab and headed to the emergency room at Lincoln Hospital. None of his teammates made the slightest attempt to take the ride with him. They no longer saw a teammate. They saw Judas. They saw a traitor. They saw a snitch. They saw a man who was responsible for their death sentences. And if that were the case, they were all dead men living on borrowed time. Without saying a word, each of them knew what needed to be done. They all needed to get out of town and keep a low profile. The goodbye hugs did not last long, but they were full of emotion. They all knew death was steps away from knocking on their doors.

"Be safe," were the last words Barkley said to each of his teammates, before he jogged off into the night. He did not look back as he jogged away. His eyes and mind were focused on the future and survival.

Chapter 15

It had been close to two weeks since Barkley went into hiding. Living in survival mode was taking a toll on his psyche as well as his physical health. Fear of retribution at the hands of the Capilini family consumed his mind over the twelve days he secluded himself from the world. He spent most of his days and nights holed up in motel rooms in Queens and Brooklyn. His attempts to diagram an escape plan were futile; because of his lack of resources—mainly financial—failure was guaranteed. With each passing day, he fell deeper into depression. Down to his last twenty dollars, he decided to go to Mother Benson's home, where he had stashed an emergency fund inside her attic. Getting that money would keep him afloat for a couple of weeks until he figured out what to do next. It was risky, but he had no other option. Resurfacing in his old Brooklyn neighborhood would be like playing Russian Roulette. Even if the Capilini's foot soldiers were not parked outside Mother Benson's house, Barkley knew the family would put a price tag on his head large enough for someone to make a phone call or carry out the hit themselves.

It was after midnight when Barkley started his trek back to Brooklyn from the Conduit Motor Inn near John F. Kennedy International Airport in Queens. He did his best to hide his appearance by putting on sunglasses and wearing a Kansas City Royals baseball cap. It was hardly inconspicuous attire, but it was all he could get his hands on. He avoided eye contact at all times. When his train arrived at the Utica Avenue station, he took three breaths, said a silent prayer, and stepped off the train. He stopped short of the exit staircase and thought what if God did not hear his first plea for guidance and cover. He began to pray again as he walked up the staircase.

"God, just in case you didn't hear me the first time, please watch out for my ass. I ain't never hurt nobody and I just wanna live. God, I just wanna live. Please keep these niggas from blasting my ass on these streets. Please, God. Amen."

Walking with tunnel vision, familiar surroundings seemed altered. The streets and blocks seemed wider and farther apart than he remembered. Running to Mother Benson's house crossed his mind, but he did not want to run into an ambush. If there was anyone waiting for him to show up at his old address, Barkley wanted to see them before they saw him. He took an indirect way to Mother Benson's to avoid any killers that may have been on the lookout for him. Going through the backyard proved to be the safest route to take, but it did come with a few scrapes from the bushes. For an individual with such an ugly personality, Mother Benson had a beautiful garden with an assortment of thorny rose bushes. Once he finally made it through the floral obstacle course, Barkley needed a helping hand from one of his former foster care siblings. His best bet for assistance was Charity and Kim. The two of them shared a room for much of their lives. Throughout their childhood, they seemed to forge a volatile and competitive relationship. For years they played the roles of mortal enemies in public. Behind closed doors, the love they shared for one another was unmatched by any love they had for anyone else. When he lived under Mother Benson's roof, Barkley would often hear the moans coming from their room as he laid awake in silence during late night hours. He didn't have to worry about being kept up all of hours of the night because Charity would usually tell Kim to shut the fuck up. There were times Kim couldn't control herself. There were even times he heard her pleasure-filled screams at full volume, which only happened when Charity couldn't get her hand to Kim's mouth in time, because she was too busy licking every nook and cranny of her lover's vagina. Once Kim reached her climax it was usually lights out for both. Tonight Barkley couldn't afford to let that happen. He picked up a few pebbles to throw toward their bedroom window and hoped one of them would look out when they heard the noise. Surprisingly, the first stone he tossed brought a halt to the couple's episode of cunnilingus. Charity quickly answered his "call."

"It's me. I need you to open the back door and let me in," Barkley said.

"For what?"

"Because if you don't, I'm not the only one who is going to know about that nice piece of ass laying next to you."

The not-so-discreet threat helped Barkley get his point across rather quickly. Charity opened the back door less than sixty seconds later. Barkley crept up the stairs and past Mother Benson's room to head to his old attic bedroom to retrieve the money he hid. Chase had taken up residence there since Barkley moved out months ago. Dealing with his snoring would be more difficult than any physical threat Chase posed if he woke up. Barkley's plan hit a snag when he opened the small compartment underneath his old bed and discovered his last lifeline was severed. The money was gone. Enraged by this monumental setback, he took it out on the first to speak a word.

"Would you hurry the fuck up," Charity said.

Her words were met with a roundhouse right to the jaw. Chase could usually sleep through anything, but the loud thump his sister made when she hit the floor immediately woke him up. Kim thought of jumping to her lover's defense. She had second thoughts after quickly comparing her size to Barkley's. Instead she took a less risky approach.

"Damn, man! Can you just get out of here and leave us alone?"

Chase was checking on his sister and didn't think to make eye contact with his sibling's attacker.

Barkley angrily paced back and forth wondering who could have taken the money. He knew Kim, Chase, and Charity were not smart enough to locate a treasure under their nose, nor were they snoopers. That left him with one door to open. It was a door he wanted to avoid at all cost. As he turned to head toward Mother Benson's bedroom, his mission to get his money back came to an abrupt end. Barkley towered over everyone in the house and could easily whip the ass of anyone he confronted. But with his back turned and a Louisville slugger to the back of the head, he was no longer the hulking figure with the upper hand. It took a couple of blows to take Barkley completely down. His violent tumble down the attic staircase compounded the effects of the homerun swing to his head. He was now unconscious.

"He was leaving. What the fuck was that about?" Chase asked.

117

The blows came from an old adversary and Mother Benson's most recent young conquest, Juvie.

"This is about getting paid and that nigga is worth a lotta cash on these streets," Juvie said.

The two adversaries hadn't come in contact with each other since the day Born stopped Juvie from breaking Barkley's legs. Juvie still harbored plenty of ill will toward Barkley and was ready to kill him on the spot. The thousands of dollars in compensation he stood to receive if he delivered Barkley breathing doused his fiery rage.

"This nigga has caused me nothing but problems since I met him. From what I hear, this piece of shit is worth five grand on the street. That's money we can all use, and if we add in what he had stored up in this house, that's a treasure I'm willing to dig in his ass to get. Believe me it won't take long. Just wail on him a little bit and get him to talk," Juvie said.

"Have you gone fucking crazy?" Chase asked.

Juvie laid out a plan, and with each word, his scheme grew more and more sinister. As Barkley lied unconsciously, Juvie made a call.

"Who was that. Who the fuck was that?" Chase asked.

Before Juvie could answer, the sound of footsteps on the first floor staircase made him pause.

"What in the hell is goin' on up here?" Mother Benson asked.

Since Barkley left, Mother Benson had softened a bit and lost some of the evil ways she showed for so many years. It was her way of coming to terms with crossing life's finish line. Her doctors had found an inoperable tumor. She had always fucked random men she knew she had no future with, and now that her life was ending she definitely was not going to pass up the opportunity to pleasure herself with a young tender in her bed. Mother Benson and Juvie had been enjoying each other's company for almost two weeks before Barkley resurfaced at the home. When the two initially met, Mother Benson thought Juvie was just looking for a sugar mama, which was a role she was happy to play. Unbeknownst to her, she was about to discover the evil intentions behind her young lover's advance. When she finally made it to the top of the stairs, her questions were still unanswered. She began to ask again but stopped in mid-sentence after she discovered her former foster child lying unconscious. She looked at Chase for answers, but got nothing in return.

"What happened to this boy? Why am I looking at what looks like a dead body in my home?" Mother Benson asked.

She started to walk toward Barkley when she was met with Juvie's second homerun swing of the night. With rage in his eyes, Juvie continued to swing, battering Mother Benson's face until it no longer had identifiable features. The visual of her dead body lying in a pool of blood was shocking to each of her remaining foster children. Chase stood frozen, paralyzed from fear and shock. When Juvie finally stopped, he turned his attention to Chase, Charity, and Kim. He attempted to joggle their minds out of the frozen state they were stuck in. First he shook Chase, then shifted his focus to Kim and Chastity. They both moved away from him, not wanting to be touched by a murderous psychopath. He tried to assure them everything would be okay, and that they would have some major currency coming their way.

"What the fuck does that mean? You playing Barry Bonds with people's heads and I'm supposed to believe you thinking clear about this shit right here? Nigga please," Charity said.

They started shouting and cursing at each other, but the insults ended abruptly when the doorbell rang.

"Don't answer that," Chase said.

"I told you I got this handled," Juvie replied.

Juvie raced down the stairs to answer the door. He stopped in the bathroom to wash Mother Benson's blood from his hands and face. The water washed over his hands, and he was not phased as the basin transformed into a whirlpool of red wine.

The bell rang again. This time it was followed by forceful knocks on the door. Once Juvie arrived at the door and checked the peephole, he opened the door and smiled as if he saw an old friend.

"What up, my niggas? Just like I said I got that package upstairs waiting for you." He stepped aside as two muscular Jamaicans walked past him to head up the stairs. Born followed them inside.

"You was right, my nigga. It was only a matter of time before that fucking fool came back home. His street IQ is most definitely lacking," Juvie said.

"Did you handle mom dukes the way we talked about? We don't need nothing messy on this one," Born said.

Juvie's delayed response angered Born. The expression of fear on his face only made his temperature rise even more. Born's plan came with easy instructions. His orchestrated scheme calling for Juvie to get in close with Mother Benson to gain access inside her home. His next step was to call Born once Barkley returned. He was then instructed to do anything he had to do to keep him at the house until Born arrived. Juvie's instructions on how to deal with Mother Benson were also laid out. He was told to lock Mother Benson in her room and to keep her there until Born arrived. In his mind the cost attached to muting Mother Benson's mouth, was a price he had no problem paying. It also kept the situation from getting complicated. However, in this situation, he did not have many more words for Juvie. Instead, he began to do the talking with his fist. His first comment was spoken by an uppercut right punch to Juvie's chin. He collapsed to the floor. He immediately got on his knees to ask for mercy like a Christian begging to be forgiven for his sins. Unfortunately for Juvie, he was not in the Lord's house, and God's forgiving nature was not something Born subscribed to.

"Motherfucka, I gave you a simple plan. Now I got a mess to clean up. Do I look like a fucking house nigga to you? Do I look like I got large supply of Mop & Glo in my fucking house?" Born asked.

As Juvie rose to his feet, he was instructed to show them the mess he had created. He took a few steps before the two enforcers with Born forcefully thrust him towards the stairs.

Born glanced over the room quickly. The blood splatter caught his attention. He masked his rage by chuckling. He slipped on Mother Benson's pool of blood, which made his chuckle turn into a full-blown eruption of laughter. His outburst of giggles didn't last long. He regained his composure, and looked at Juvie.

"Filet that bitch ass nigga," Born said.

His marching order was executed in a matter of

seconds. One of his two Jamaican henchmen grabbed Juvie from behind and slit his throat in one swift motion. Chase, Kim, and Charity were horrified by the violent end of Juvie's life and Born was now faced with a dilemma. On top of the two dead bodies, he also had three loose ends. Killing the remaining witnesses would just bring a shit storm of press and police. Two dead bodies in the same place was nothing out of the ordinary in that part of Brooklyn, but five dead bodies would be front-page news for a week. Murder was no longer on Born's mind when he told Charity, Kim, and Chase to strip down to their skivvies. All three of them began to beg for mercy. Born's enforcers waved guns in each person's direction as they rushed them to strip down to their underwear. They all waited to hear the gunshot that would end it all. To their surprise, they were spared.

"I want y'all to listen and listen very fucking carefully. When the police and fire trucks come, y'all don't know shit. All you know is you woke up and smoke was everywhere and you got the fuck out. You keep quiet about this and y'all will get what I was about to give that dumb motherfucker, Juvie," Born said.

Chase, Kim, and Charity all agreed to keep quiet. They didn't know what was about to happen until they began to smell gas. As Born was laying out his new plan to mask the bloodshed inside the house, his two soldiers were setting up a homemade bomb that would erase evidence of everything that happened that night. The burners on the oven shot gas throughout the house. Once Barkley's unconscious body was picked up off the floor, the fuse on the makeshift explosive was lit. It took a couple of minutes for everyone to exit the house in the backyard. Moments later, an explosion tore through the home. Born released a sigh of relief, knowing the mess he walked into was now cleaned up. The death toll was higher, but his connection to Barkley's return to Brooklyn was severed. He instructed his goons to take Barkley to the car. His old friend was still unconscious, but he had enough life in him to guarantee his time on Earth was not up.

Chapter 16

As Barkley began to awaken from his coma-like state, he immediately felt the aftermath of the bat bashing his head. His vision was blurry, but he was able to gather a few descriptive components of the room he awoke in. Mister Vegas' "Gallis" blaring from speakers inside a nearby house instantly provided enough information for him to pinpoint his location. There weren't many places in the city where dancehall tunes could be heard early in the morning. He knew he was Brooklyn. Fearful that sunlight or any sort of illumination would accentuate the pain stemming from his blunt force trauma, Barkley kept his distance from the window. He did his best to walk gingerly across the wooden floor, but the old house made squeaky noises. He did not have much of an escape plan in mind, nor did he know if he should try to escape. The fact he was still breathing made him wonder if his life was in danger. Maybe he was in good company, and had nothing to fear. That flash of optimism quickly subsided, when he began working up several different scenarios in his brain. Each scenario ended with his violent death, which was a conclusion he wanted no parts of. Barkley was now back in survival mode and living another day was his objective. Opening the room door was too much of a noisy option. His escape needed to be a covert operation so he decided to take a leap of faith from the window. It was a gutsy move, and one that could not be executed from the second floor of a brownstone without incurring serious injury. Barkley made his way over to the window to check out the lay of the land as well as the degree of difficulty he faced. His attempt at a silent escape ended abruptly when his slight tug on the shade caused it to roll all the way up, blasting him with a ray of sunlight that made him retreat back to his starting point. He stumbled towards the bed he awoke in and covered his eyes with his hands, hoping to quickly repair his eyes from the blinding sun.

As he began to remove his hands from his eyes, the spaces between his fingers gave him his first look at the men who were responsible for getting him to his current location. The two burly Jamaican enforcers stood silently staring at Barkley.

"What the fuck is going on? I didn't have anything to do with that shit!" Barkley said.

"Oh, yes you did," Born said as he walked in the room.

The appearance of his old friend shocked Barkley. The jolt made him very nervous. Barkley did not know if Born was standing before him ready to hit the kill switch on his life, or if he was there to save him as he always had in the past.

The seconds of silence seemed everlasting and Barkley thought the worst.
Born observed the beads of sweat trickling down Barkley's face. The sight of him looking panicked made him chuckle. With a smirk on his face, Born broke the silence.

"Look at this shivering bitch. Whatever is going through your head, I want you to keep it there because that is what's gonna keep you alive. You're safe behind these walls, but out there... the vultures are circling and it's only a matter of time before they chow down on that ass."

"What am I doing here? My life is in danger and

you talking in riddles," Barkley said

"Riddles, huh?" Born straddled a nearby chair and let out a deep breath. He was about to launch into the story of Barkley's teammates' demise. The stories of their deaths came attached with graphic details. His first tale was the tragic death of Man Child and his family.

"Family? Wait, what the fuck did they have to do with anything?" Barkley asked.

"Dog, you guys clearly weren't thinking when y'all agreed to do this shit for ya boy. What part of fucking over an Italian mafia family sounded like good ass idea to you?" Born asked.

It wasn't as if Barkley wasn't warned about dealing with Kevlar. His naiveté is what angered Born the most and he knew Barkley would end up in some form of trouble or six feet under. Born was ready to help, but first he wanted give a vivid description of what Barkley was facing and what had become of his teammates. He felt Man Child got off easy because he was first and didn't see his end coming. To a normal civilian on the street, a story about a family involved in a head on collision with privately owned garbage truck was just an unfortunate accident. Folks making their bread in the belly of the beast or anyone with a high degree of street knowledge could see right through the accident report. Everybody knew the Italian crime families ran the private garbage pick-up industry. Everyone also knew it was a truck owned by the Capilini family that was involved in the fatal smash-up. The word was out. There was a green light on Kevlar and anyone connected to Bk To Tha Fullest, which meant players, Moncrief and anybody with them when it came time to hit that kill switch was also going to be taken down in the same violent fashion.

Man Child's son and his lady died on impact. Unfortunately for him, it took much more than a collision with an enormous garbage truck to take him out. The car exploded shortly after the impact. The raging flames closed the deal on his life, roasting his body until it became charred remains.

The twins were next to turn up in the morgue. Their murders were carried out almost a week after the game. Double-Double wanted to hit the Casper Lounge one last night before heading out of town. Their last night there would be their last on Earth. Those two were always running a train on women. They'd been tossing back drinks all night before they met the voluptuous Dominican woman they targeted. Each brother let their fingers do the talking, groping her ass and breasts. With each touch she seemed to like it more and more. The brothers sensed the night was going to be special. From the way the situation was playing out, they even stopped planning their normal routine of secretly changing places after climaxing. Instead of taking the chick back to their place, they decided to oblige the woman's request and do her in their SUV. Thirty minutes later, police found her bloodied and bruised with both brothers dead in the back seat wearing nothing but their socks. Both were cut up with blood leaking from multiple stab wounds. The brothers' sexual conquest did not look like a knife-wielding double murderer, nor did she carry the appearance of an innocent victim, but she cooked up a great story that allowed her to mask her true involvement in the killings. Teary-eyed and shivering, she told police things got out of control when her jealous ex-boyfriend and his crew showed up. According to her well-rehearsed story, the backseat threesome was about to go down when her former jilted lover pulled up. The name she gave was Hector Velazquez.

"Now I've heard of motherfuckers making contact with their lady after they've passed. You know, that Patrick Swayze shit. But I ain't never heard of a nigga coming back from the dead to murder niggas about to give their girl some dick," Born said.

According to Born, Capilini family soldiers escorted Hector Velazquez out of Latin Quarters in a drunken mess two months ago and made him vanish. He was an illegal immigrant experiencing the American dream, all the result of him running a lucrative cocaine operation for the Capilinis in Paterson, New Jersey. Nobody had seen him since that night, and with word out that he was skimming off the top of the cocaine shipments, all signs pointed to a violent Capilini family-style deportation.

Officially, the details behind the deaths of Double-Double connected Velazquez as the prime suspect, thanks to a very believable story from the woman paid to set them up.

"What's sad about that whole situation is them niggas thought they were about to stab some pussy before going on the run but wound up getting stabbed to death because they thought with their dicks. Pussy karma is real," Born said.

He continued, telling Barkley the twins never even got to pull their dicks out. A Capilini execution crew followed them to the desolate area they selected for the threesome. They rushed the van and ripped the brothers to shreds. When police arrived, they found fingers and one eye scattered near the twins' car and a battered woman

128

singing a concocted story of her crazy ex-boyfriend's murderous rampage. The body count was at three and the Capilini family was on course to finish off Kevlar and his team by Christmas.

When word got out about the twins, Khakalak knew it was only a matter of time before the grim reaper showed up at his door. He ran for as long as he could muster the strength, but deep down inside he knew he wasn't built to live a life of looking over his shoulder. Most on the streets knew the same, which is why everyone thought he'd be first to get put in a coffin. He proved a lot of people wrong; no one thought he would take himself out.

"Gotta give the country bastard credit. He went out the way he wanted to," Born said.

The prostitute told police he seemed happy after she rode his dick until his orgasmic eruption. She said he gave the impression he was in good spirits as he spent about an hour after climaxing talking about all sorts of ambitions. He talked about going home and seeing his mom and dad before he strolled into the bathroom. The mention of his parents would have been a red flag to those who knew Khakalak, since he only spoke of them when revealing they were dead. The French Canadian working girl from the escort service waited for forty-five minutes before she began to call out to Khakalak. She said she genuinely liked him because he was the first customer who ever made her feel like Julia Roberts in the film Pretty Woman. Khakalak gave her an experience she'd never had on any of her dates. His manners extended past their introduction, which was rare for women working as escorts. She became concerned when Khakalak was unresponsive to her calls. She even made a request for more sex—free of charge—

and there was still no answer. Unable to ignore the silence any longer, she gave three hard knocks to the door and opened the door. Just as the doors swung ajar, Khakalak fired a bullet into his killing himself instantly. The gruesome end of his life made the woman scream loud enough to be heard on the entire eighth floor inside the midtown Holiday Inn. Compared to the locations and methods of murder carried out on his teammates, Khakalak's decision to end his life moments after getting some pussy at a swanky hotel didn't make his death any less tragic to Barkley.

"At least he got to choose where he took his last breath," Barkley said.

"Your coach Moncrief, now that's a nigga I feel for," Born said.

"Ah, damn, Moncrief! He wasn't even in on the shit."

"Nigga, they knew that, but if any motherfucker was at the wrong place at the wrong time, it was that nigga time to go just like the motherfucker being targeted," Born said.

From the moment the referee tossed up the jump ball at the game with the Russians, the clock started ticking on Moncrief's life. When his clock expired, he was staring down the barrel of a sawed off shotgun and didn't even have a clue what was coming his way. He and Kevlar were taken out at the same time. Moncrief showed up at Kevlar's brownstone in Bed-Stuy looking for answers. The meeting was set up after Kevlar finally agreed to meet up with his former coach. Paranoia consumed Kevlar, along with streaks of frustration, generated by his inability to determine who was playing the role of friend or foe in his life. Moncrief wanted to know why his players were turning up dead and Kevlar was the man with answers.

Moncrief didn't have to wait long for Kevlar to answer the door. The door opened with the chain latch attached after the second knock. Once he realized it was a friendly face behind the door, Kevlar repeatedly asked Moncrief, if he'd been followed. He asked if anyone saw him get out his car. It was five in the morning and Moncrief did not respond nicely to the barrage of questions Kevlar was throwing at him. It would have continued if Moncrief hadn't demanded the door be opened.

"Open this fucking door, man. You either on some shit or you're in some deep shit. Either way I'm here to help and find out what the hell is going on," Moncrief said.

When he finally opened the door, Kevlar felt at ease as he embraced the only person he could trust. But in that instance his fears came to reality. His violent end had come to pass. It was death by ambush. With guns drawn, six Capilini soldiers ran towards the house firing a barrage of bullets. Gunfire to the legs took down Kevlar and Moncrief. Two days prior to his death, the Capilini family began following Moncrief everywhere he went. He had no clue he was being tailed over the last 48 hours when he showed up to Kevlar's home. Once the crew of executioners spotted Kevlar they immediately began spraying their targets with hollow point ammunition. The lives of both men ended with a shotgun blast to the face. Blood splattered all over the front stoop, leaving evidence of a gruesome, professionally executed murder. Payback was written all over it. Now, Barkley was the only one left.

Barkley sat in silence as numbness consumed his body. After hearing about the demise of his team, his mind churned out several violent death scenarios. He envisioned himself at the receiving end of a Capilini firing squad. His mind even created scenarios where Born's goons beat him to death. His death squad scenarios stopped playing out in his head when someone rang the doorbell.

"The keys to your future have just arrived my friend," Born said.

Unaware of what was awaiting him, Barkley jumped up to plead for his friend's help. He attempted to follow Born out of the room, but was stopped and restrained. As Born's two-man security force held him down, Barkley listened out for any clues that could give him signs of what was coming his way. He only heard two sets of footsteps on the staircase. He managed to lift his head off the ground enough to see one pair of the footsteps belonged to someone from his past that had a lot of practice saving his ass. It was Harrison.

"You here to kill me too, man?" Barkley yelled.

"I'm here to clean up the fucking mess your life has become. I could get whacked for not putting a bullet in your head. Your boy's life and his entire operation are at stake right now. So you're gonna listen to what the fuck I have to say and do whatever the fuck I want you to do. That's if you want to stay alive past Christmas," Harrison said.

Harrison corroborated all of Born's story. The Capilini family took a major hit to their finances following the game with the Russians, and a price had to paid by everyone who was responsible for that. Barkley was a dead man if he stayed in New York. It was that cut and dry. His only two friends were casting a lifeline to him and the only way to keep breathing was to grab hold of it and carry out the escape plan Harrison had in mind.

Barkley stayed holed up in Harrison's two bedroom apartment over the next three days. His pad was pristine with enough technical gadgets and guns that would make most think he was a violent geek. On the day Harrison selected to carry out his plan into his guestroom door startling Barkley.

"It's time, young buck. Yo' ass got a one way ticket out of here and it's time to punch it," Harrison said.

The exit strategy Harrison laid out didn't sit too well with Barkley, but it was the only game plan that was going to keep him alive. Harrison's plan called for Barkley to board an Albany, New York-bound bus in the Queens Village section of Queens. From there, he'd hop on a bus to Cleveland, Ohio. Once he arrived, one of the few men Harrison trusted would be there to pick him up. Harrison told Barkley he would learn the rest from his pick-up driver. It was a somber moment when they arrived at the bus depot. As Barkley took steps toward the bus entrance, Harrison pulled him back. With a stern look on his face, he launched into a verbal tirade laced with emotion and warnings. The dialogue he delivered went straight to the point.

"Listen to what the fuck I gotta say. You are alive because people cared enough about you to put their own lives on the line. Don't do anything that will put them at the bottom of a hole with regrets about helping your naive ass. You fucking hear me? Now get your ass on the bus."

As Barkley walked up the steps onto the bus he looked back at the man who entered his life as a mentor and later became his saving grace. He sat in his seat staring upward with thoughts of living another day, even months.

These were thoughts he couldn't fathom forty-eight hours earlier.

Chapter 17

Twenty hours after his departure from the Big Apple, Barkley arrived in Cleveland, Ohio. The city felt nothing like New York. The concrete jungle he called home had been replaced by a city fast asleep until its alarm clock went off just before sunrise. Barkley exited the bus with three other weary travelers. The two parents and their pre-teen daughter quickly disappeared along with the bus, leaving him alone in an empty lot. He briefly wondered if Harrison had put him on a bus to be whacked in a city foreign to him to keep his hands clean and his conscious clear. The absence of transport from his pick-up point produced a tornado of tangents in Barkley's brain. It spun in every direction imaginable until he saw a sign. Flashing high beams brought an abrupt end to the mind-altering twister, and were immediately followed by a blaring horn. Barkley began walking toward the car. He was knee-deep in worry, so his turtle like pace did not sit well with the driver who called him over. The man behind the wheel thought he could hasten Barkley's step by turning on his interior lighting. The light shining from the roof of the car revealed a skinny white man with a bald patch down the middle of his head, surrounded by silver remnants of his once full head of hair.

"Yo, Gaucho, is that you?" Barkley asked.

The opening car door was not the response Barkley was looking for. A war of thoughts broke out in his head. He didn't know if he should continue to wait for an answer or make a run for it. The battle waged on as the mysterious white man dressed in mechanic's overalls walked his way. Barkley was two feet away from the stranger when his question was answered.

"I'm Gaucho but if I wasn't you'd be just another dead nigger on the streets of Cleveland, courtesy of the Capilini family. You've got a lot to learn about hiding out and staying hidden."

Barkley wanted some answers about his transporter. He asked a barrage of questions that went unanswered. Gaucho thought it was best at that time. The two men knew only one thing about each other: Harrison was the only man they trusted with their lives. They returned to Gaucho's car and began their journey to Sandusky.

Driving made Gaucho more relaxed around Barkley. He even loosened his lips to entertain some questions. The hour ride west on Interstate 90 didn't produce all the answers Barkley wanted. However, it did set up the perfect *getting to know you* session for both Barkley and Gaucho. The conversation revealed a lot of commonalities between Barkley and the newest member of his rescue team. Gaucho seemed to be more excited about having a fellow New Yorker in his car more than anything else. His motor mouth made nodding off to sleep impossible so Barkley listened as Gaucho disclosed the reason behind his banishment from the Big Apple in a staccato-like fashion. He was lucky if he understood every other word uttered from Gaucho's mouth. His story also unveiled information about Harrison Barkley never knew. After piecing the words together, Barkley learned Gaucho was an ex-wise guy snitch for Harrison. He helped Harrison move up the ranks with information leading to the arrests of key Gambino crime family members. Harrison's police work made him a NYPD rock star. Gaucho became a man with valuable information by bartending at the Boot Lounge. Working at the mobster hang out provided Gaucho with tidbits of information about deals and beefs amongst most of the New York City-based families. Once attached to some police work, Harrison turned those small rations of information into full course meals for prosecutors. Gaucho provided information on the Capilini family, but Harrison never moved on those leads. His lack of motivation on Capilini affairs did not raise flags at One Police Plaza. The higher ups were not going to tear Harrison a new asshole just because it seemed one New Jersey-based family was not on his radar. Barkley did not follow suit. He wanted to learn the origin of Harrison's relationship with the Capilini family.

"I know a few things about our buddy Detective Harrison that could get him dinosaur years in prison. But I would never turn on him because of his loyalty even when his own life is in jeopardy," Gaucho said before beginning his story.

While he didn't get any flak from his superiors over his lack of Capilini collars, he did net some benefits from looking the other way. Curious as to why he kept mum on information he received pertaining to the Capilini family, Harrison was called in for his first of many meetings with the boss, Vincent Capilini. This sit down had the feel of a high stakes poker game. However in this case, both sides were willing to show their hands just to see how the other wanted to benefit. All Harrison wanted was forgiveness for a very important family member. His uncle Barry had accrued massive gambling debts with the Capilini family over the last fifteen years. Uncle Barry would win some, but he lost most other times. Paying off the Capilini family was a slow death for Uncle Barry. He didn't have the cash and he no longer had the youth to execute a big score. Sensing the demise of the man who raised him, Harrison orchestrated a plan to get in close with the Capilinis. The blueprint of the scheme called for Harrison to turn over key information on investigations targeting them. In return, Vincent would agree to the forfeiture of Uncle Barry's debt. Both sides reaped huge benefits from the deal. With a firm handshake, they began a business arrangement that kept key Capilini family members out of prison, and Harrison's uncle out of the cemetery.

"So where do you fit in all of this?" Barkley asked.

"I'm getting to that. I'm a little long-winded with my stories," Gaucho said.

Harrison wasn't the only cop the Capilini family had in their back pocket. However, he did prove to be the one they could depend on the most.

The more Harrison worked with the Capilinis the more everything in his world turned gray. Black and white lines were blurred, and Harrison eventually became the muscle for the Capilini family. His promotion to narcotics detective allowed him to work the streets and stay off the radar when he spent his working hours punishing individuals targeted by the Capilinis.

If giving the Capilinis a heads up on investigations was a walk in the park, assassinating his number one informant was the one ride Harrison never wanted to get on. The agreement with the Capilinis spanned five years before he was ordered to kill Gaucho.

"Why did they want you dead?" Barkley asked.

"I saw something I wasn't supposed to see," Gaucho said.

The life-changing event happened close to a decade ago, but Gaucho remembered like it occurred the same day he picked up Barkley. The events played out in his head as he told Barkley his story. Gaucho followed his regular routine that frigid December night. He was bartending, and hoping to get the place closed on time and get out earlier than usual, he became a one man cleaning crew. He wiped down the bar and tables, and even insisted on taking out the garbage to the back alley. There, he heard the faint sound of a man moaning, which piqued his interest. It was normal for intoxicated bar patrons to make their way to a secluded section of the alley for business transactions with the local hookers. But this was in December, and the curiosity behind who was getting their dick polished outside in 20-degree weather was pulling at Gaucho too much for him not to take a look. Once he got a glimpse of where the pleasure-filled moans originated from, he knew it was in his best interest to get the hell out of there. Two men engaged in sex was the last visual Gaucho thought he would see. He cursed himself for being nosy, not for what he saw, but for who he saw. Witnessing Vincent Capilini's first born son, Arturo taking a black man's dick up his ass would put Gaucho at the top of a hit list. As Gaucho scurried away, a rat ran between his legs. Startled, he lost his balance and stumbled into the view of Arturo and his male lover. Time froze once the men locked eyes. Gaucho was the first to break away from the trance.

"I got the fuck out of there so fast. There was no way Arturo Capilini was gonna let me keep breathing, knowing what I knew," Gaucho said.

Harrison was the first person Gaucho called for help. Both knew there was only one way he'd avoid suffering the wrath of Arturo: by getting the hell out of New York City. They devised a plan that put both of their lives in jeopardy. A few days passed before Gaucho met with Arturo and his dad, Vincent. There was only one topic of discussion and that was taking out Gaucho. Harrison was only told Gaucho got wind of some information they couldn't afford to let get out. The heir to the Capilini organized crime operation joyfully taking a black cock up his ass was definitely a secret the family would spare no expense to keep buried. Knowing he was the only person who could keep Gaucho alive, Harrison convinced the Capilinis to let him handle the kill contract. His track record with the family gave Harrison credibility. He'd come through for them in the past, and no one would suspect a cop of taking out a bartender who worked at the Boot Lounge.

"He didn't kill you. So how did Harrison show the Capilinis he held up his end of the deal?" Barkley asked.

Gaucho thought it'd be better to show his new hideout partner how he pulled off his disappearing act rather than tell him.

He took control of the wheel with his right hand, while using his mouth to pull off his left glove. Gaucho's missing pinky said it all.

Harrison had provided evidence of Gaucho's demise then gave him a one-way ticket to Sandusky, Ohio. Gaucho knew the area because he had spent several summers working at Cedar Point Amusement Park.

For Gaucho, there were no emotional goodbyes to the Big Apple. He wanted to live, and if it meant losing a pinky and leaving the city in his rearview, that was fine with him.

Suddenly, Gaucho stopped talking about New York and switched to someone named Betty, a woman he met a few months after he arrived in Sandusky. She fell for his New York City swagger. He fell for her bedroom tricks and the magic she worked in the kitchen.

Gaucho's life no longer mirrored the edge of a waterfall. New surroundings and new love made his life complete. He was now floating on a stream, and wanted to keep the ripples to a minimum, but taking in Barkley threatened to turn his stream into roaring rapids. But, just as his life had been saved, he decided to return the favor. Barkley listened respectfully to Gaucho's story, but what he heard over the last ten miles of the trip made him think about returning to New York to take his chances. Gaucho began to lay out how life would be for the next few months. Barkley did not waste a moment expressing his disapproval of the survival plan set for him.

"To keep you busy and out of trouble, I've set up an appointment at Sandusky Memorial High School. We don't have any paperwork for you, but I've got a hook up that can get you enrolled until we figure out what our next step is," Gaucho said.

"Get the fuck outta here. School and me never got along, and I damn sure ain't trying to make up now," said Barkley.

They argued, reaching a fevered pitch with threats from both sides. Gaucho did his best to make it clear it was his way or the highway. Barkley responded with comments that amounted to him not giving a fuck what his new acquaintance said. The arguing stopped when Gaucho suggested they continue talking later that day.

"I don't give a fuck when we talk about it. Morning, noon, or night, I ain't changing my mind on this shit. We gotta find another plan," Barkley said.

Knowing how his lady hated to be in the company of conflict, Gaucho shut down the arguing for the sake of Betty. He pulled into the driveway of the small house with the brick exterior. The block of similar styled homes was very quiet, which was extremely foreign to Barkley.

The sun had completely risen by the time they entered the home. The smell of freshly cooked eggs, bacon, biscuits, and hash browns signified breakfast time. Barkley was stunned by the amount of food on the table at 7 a.m. Back in Brooklyn, Mother Benson hardly ever cooked anything. There were times he was amazed the oven burners worked. Betty often cooked, but she made sure to give her newest houseguest the red carpet treatment to make him feel at home.

"How was your trip?" Betty asked.

Barkley couldn't utter a word before Betty had him in her arms. She stood a few inches south of five feet, so her arms wrapped around Barkley's frame just above his waist. An uncomfortable smirk surfaced on his face as he looked down, then across to Gaucho. He wasn't used to middle-aged white women embracing him, but he went with it.

"The trip was long. I'm happy to be off that bus," Barkley said.

"I bet you are. I'm sure seeing your uncle was a great sight."

Barkley erupted into laughter at Betty's comment, but he played along with Gaucho's story line. If she didn't become suspicious of her boyfriend having a black nephew, he wasn't going to give her any reason to question the story she was told.

"Yea, seeing Old Uncle G brought back great memories," Barkley said.

"Uncle G? What does the G stand for Clarence?" Betty asked, turning to Gaucho.

"It's short for a name the guys in the neighborhood called me," Gaucho said.

After a few minutes of non-stop pestering, Betty learned her Clarence, was better known as Gaucho before she met him. Satisfied with the answers to her multiple questions, Betty planted a kiss on Gaucho, then left the house as she normally did 7:30 a.m. every morning to open up her bakery.

Tension between Barkley and Gaucho built with each passing minute as they rapidly ate their breakfast in silence. Gaucho walked outside to smoke a cigarette. He would've stayed inside, but he needed to get some space between himself and Barkley. Just looking in the direction of his bone-headed houseguest made Gaucho fantasize about using one of Betty's frying pans to get his point across. He paced on the porch back and forth and wound up smoking the two remaining cigarettes in his pack of Newport. His final cigarette nearly burned to the filter when he came up with an idea: Barkley could work at the shop. Gaucho would have to come up with a good explanation for why his nephew wasn't in school, but he'd come up with good lies to tell Betty before. As he went to open the door, Barkley beat him to the knob on the other side of the screen door.

"Fuck it. I'll do it your way," Barkley said.

While Gaucho mulled different scenarios in his head, Barkley was doing some thinking of his own. He thought it would be best to learn about surviving rather than going his own way this time. Gaucho managed to build a pretty good life for himself while he was on the run, Barkley realized as he sat in Betty's dining room. If he was going to learn how to stay alive, playing the role of a high school student was only going to help his lessons go over much smoother. They confirmed their agreement with a handshake. The first step was acceptance. The second step in Gaucho's plan nearly made Barkley reverse his decision.

"Hell no, I ain't dying my hair. What the fuck I wanna look like Sisqo or Chris Brown for?" Barkley asked.

"Young fella, if you wanna become someone different you gotta look different. Believe me, it helps with the transformation."

Barkley admitted he was a bit worried about taking on a new identity. He didn't think he could play the role of high school kid in a convincing fashion after living in a grown-up world for the past few months, but before the end of the night Barkley was a blond.

Chapter 18

The alarm clock buzzer sent shockwaves through Barkley's body the next morning. Waking up at 7 a.m. was going to take some getting used to. He attempted to hit the snooze button, but his hand was slapped away by the bright-eyed and bushy-tailed white lady of the house. Betty made certain Barkley was up and ready to get going on his first day of school. She pushed him toward the shower, and shortly after that, to the breakfast table. Betty informed Barkley that would be their routine until he could do it on his own. She kissed him and Gaucho on the cheek before heading to her shop. Once she left, the conversation shifted to Barkley's new identity. Gaucho spoke with Harrison about new documents for Barkley, but the delivery was delayed because it was an out-of-state job. For the time being, they'd have to wing it.

"So who am I going to become?" Barkley asked.

"Sebastian Caminzo," Gaucho replied.

"Fuck kinda name is that?"

"It's yours, and since Harrison has already placed the order, you gotta deal with it."

With no documents, they needed to bullshit the school officials to get a grace period. In the car ride to Sandusky Memorial High School, Gaucho and Barkley worked on turning Sebastian Caminzo into a real person that was real enough to throw off any suspicion of shady practices. When they pulled up to the school, Barkley got a clear picture of how people lived on the other side of the tracks. He'd seen nice schools in New York, but nothing like Sandusky. The grass was manicured with the school logo emblazoned on the football field. The entrance of the school was pristine with landscaping plus blue and yellow floral arrangements to show off school colors. When Barkley arrived inside the building, he noticed everyone was happy. The hallways were filled with kids who looked like they didn't want to be anywhere else in the world. Each student in the hall had a smile on his or her face. Inside the administration office, he and Gaucho were assisted right away. To Barkley's surprise, they didn't have to blow much smoke up the asses of school officials. They understood how luggage got lost and would give them a grace period of one week to get the documents. In less than an hour, Barkley Capleton was history. Sebastian Caminzo was assigned his course schedule and sent to Ms. Jordan's 12th grade English class. Sebastian took his time, taking in his new surroundings with each step. When he finally arrived at Ms. Jordan's class, he stood outside the door looking in. Initially it was fear of not knowing what he was walking into, but then that turned into admiration of the startling beauty standing before him. Ms. Jordan walked to the head of the class and called for order. She got every student's attention, including Sebastian's.

Felicia Jordan's English class caused Sebastian to take a new vested interest in school. His newfound interest was not wrapped up in his love for literary greats or Ms. Jordan's lesson plan. His focus was purely on his teacher. His eyes locked on the chocolate skin tone of the African goddess standing on the other side of the door. Her body was draped in a loose fitting floral patterned dress, but it did nothing to hide the plump derriere flourishing from her hips. Ms. Jordan could grace the pages of *Playboy* or *King* magazine, but he could tell she was the type of woman who had aspirations greater than showing off her body. The combination of beauty and brains coupled with her sweet voice commanded Sebastian's attention as she gave instructions to the class. Suddenly, she glanced towards the door and greeted Sebastian's stare with a smile. She motioned him to come in the classroom. Upon entering, it seemed all eyes became fixed on Sebastian in a synchronized motion.

"Can I help you? From the look on your face, you seem to be a little lost," Ms. Jordan said.

Sebastian looked over the room before reaching for the document with his class schedule. He locked eyes with many of the elite students he knew he'd never cross paths with in New York. The stare down would have been intimidating to most, but Sebastian could care less about the unspoken thoughts circling the minds of his new classmates.

"Oh, so you're a newbie. Well, class, we've got a rookie in our midst. Let's withhold the hazing until next week," Ms. Jordan said.

Sebastian's infatuation became much greater in that instance. A woman with a sense of humor intrigued him. She had him at the word newbie. He sat in the empty seat two rows away from Ms. Jordan. However, he had every intention of getting closer to her in more ways than one.

Sebastian had reached the middle of the school day when he sat down for lunch in the cafeteria. The new kid label usually came with its fair share of stares, but Sebastian felt eyes in every direction. He wasn't the only black student, nor was he one of a small group. The school's black and brown population was large enough for

Sebastian to fit in, but he failed to feel any attachment to them. He sat alone for much of his lunch break in the cafeteria until someone named Xavier sat next to him. Startled a little bit by the arrival of the short Korean kid with cornrows, Sebastian welcomed the company. Xavier had more than a few questions, but when he didn't get any answers, he changed his approach. He made himself the focal point of the conversation. Over a span of ten minutes, Sebastian learned Xavier's popularity in school was largely due to his role as the manager of the school basketball team. He had dreams of suiting up, but his height and lack of athletic ability made his goal unlikely. Sebastian felt a connection with Xavier once he discovered they both had an undying love for basketball. They spent the next twenty-five minutes debating the games of Derrick Rose and Dwayne Wade, and arguing over who represented Chicago ballers the best. They stopped when the lunch period ended and the school security guard broke the conversation up. Xavier invited Sebastian to continue the dialogue at the school basketball team's practice after school. Sebastian agreed, but before they departed he wanted to know why Xavier decided to sit next to him.

"Do you sit next all the new students at lunch? What made you come over here?"

"I saw your sneakers. I knew you were a baller and an all-around cool ass mofo if you had on the Air Jordan 6's."

Sebastian could only smile. His new Asian friend might have some street knowledge. He wasn't like anyone he'd known in New York, but he was happy Xavier could relate to an aspect of the culture he grew up in.

JAMAL A. BENJAMIN

Chapter 19

The Sandusky Storm Raiders were not a nationally ranked powerhouse on America's high school basketball landscape, but they were the hottest ticket in town for the locals. Christian Cerano led the team into their battles on the hardwood for the last three years. Everyone in town viewed him as the can't-miss kid. It was NBA or bust for the Italian with the sweet jumper. He basked in the glory of being the latest Cerano to lace up his sneakers and don the Storm Raiders uniform. The long-range game was what Christian's father and his uncles were most known for. Anyone with that last name was known for shooting the lights out whenever they stepped on the court. There wasn't a place on the court where making a jump shot would be a problem for a member of the Cerano family, and Christian kept that legacy alive. Unfortunately for some of the students at Sandusky, Christian also followed the family tradition of being an asshole star athlete. Being pampered and privileged paved the way for him to follow in those infamous footsteps. Being a Cerano came with a pass that got Christian out of jail, detention, classes, and whatever shit storm he could conjure up.

Sebastian walked into the gymnasium as the Storm Raiders were concluding practice. He didn't get there early enough to see who had game, but he did get there in time to witness Cerano attempting to clown his new buddy.

Xavier lacked the basketball skills to make the team. He took the role as team manager to be next to the action. Team manager was a great achievement for Xavier, but he was nothing more than a glorified water boy to the players who had fun humiliating and embarrassing him on a consistent basis. Christian was the chief prankster on the team, and his target was Xavier the majority of the time. Fully aware of how much Xavier would love to get into a game, Christian challenged him to a game of H.O.R.SE. There were past incidents where Xavier fell victim to Christian's cruel intentions, but this time he vowed the jock would have to find another sucker to be the punch line for his practical joke. Xavier stuck to his guns until Christian started waving the one carrot stick he always treasured.

"Come on, man. I'll make it fair. If you make me get H, I'll have coach put you on the roster for the next game. You know I can make that happen. Just one letter, and you're suiting up," Christian said.

The offer was too good to refuse. Xavier took the bait.

"Bet. Now if you lose, I get to throw the rock at your buck ass naked five times," Christian said.

Once the contest started, it didn't take long for him to realize this was just another one of Christian's jokes. Standing 6'2", dunking the ball was an easy shot for Christian to make. Unfortunately for Xavier, his lack of jumping ability and his 5'5" frame made leaping above the rim nothing but a pipe dream. A two-handed backwards dunk followed by a one-handed slam left Xavier with only three more chances to save himself from ultimate embarrassment. He began to silently pray for the team's coach to return from his office to save him. He quickly realized his prayers went unanswered when Christian gave him his third letter with a two-handed dunk. With H-O-R already in his column, two more missed shots would mean game over for Xavier. He was about given his second to last letter when a hesitant hero answered his prayer.

Sebastian wanted to be the new kid who stayed out of trouble, but that was no longer an option once he observed the idiotic jock bullying the first person who reached out to him. Sebastian didn't pick the best way to intervene, but nonetheless he launched a basketball toward the back of Christian's head. It was all he could come up with. Hitting the school's basketball star with a Spaulding as he was about to execute one of his dunks, catapulted him into the middle of a situation that would be problematic for his low profile. Avoiding drama should have been easy, but Sebastian felt a lesson needed to be taught to the jokester who wanted to throw a basketball at Xavier's naked ass just for kicks.

"I see you guys like to fuck around with the help, but me personally, I like to fuck around with money, and my money says I can whip the pretty boy's ass in a one on one game. First one to three wins, and I'll even make it fair. I'll play barefoot," Barkley said.

"I would love to take your funds, but I don't play for food stamps," Christian said.

"Do you play for Benjamins?" Barkley pressed.

For a brief moment it was like a vow of silence swept through the gymnasium. "So do we have a bet? Winner takes all. One hundred dollars on the line."

"Sure, I'll take your money, and I want those Jordans."

This was an expensive wager for Sebastian. He hardly knew Xavier, but teaching Christian a lesson was driving him to put it all on the line. Once he agreed to the bet, pandemonium erupted. The cheerleaders practicing nearby shut down their exercise routine to check out what the entire ruckus was about. The basketball squad members grew excited over the challenge levied against their team leader.

Xavier rushed over to Sebastian to ask what most inside the gymnasium were thinking. "What the hell are you doing? Unless your feet were made by Nike, why would you make a bet like that?"

"I got this, X-man. Just hold my shoes and watch me make this money."

With his bare feet under him, Sebastian walked to the foul line dribbling the ball. He gave Christian an intense stare before thrusting the ball from his chest toward his adversary.

"Game on," said Sebastian.

Christian dribbled the ball to his left. He bounced the ball through his legs before going for his signature move, the crossover dribble. Sebastian saw that coming a mile away. He swiped the ball away just as easy as if he were taking a ball from an infant.

Christian was now on defense. He attempted to swipe the ball away from Sebastian but once he lunged for it, that quickly became his downfall. Sebastian spun off his defender's back and dribbled toward the basket for an easy lay-up.

"That's one. Check the ball," Sebastian said.

Christian checked the ball in and was about to begin some trash talk, but Sebastian's jump shot shut that down. The ball rained down through the net without hitting the rim. Christian was now one point away from experiencing his own embarrassment. His nervousness made him a shaky defender. He reacted to every move Sebastian made. Well aware he had his adversary in the palm of his hand, Sebastian faked a jump shot, which sent Christian flying in the air. Once Sebastian got Christian airborne, Sebastian strolled in for another lay-up. In less than two minutes, he made one hundred dollars and turned the tables on the most popular student in school. His low profile was dead and gone. Everyone was going to want to know about the new kid, especially the school basketball coach, who just witnessed his star player get his ass served to him.

As he put on his sneakers, Sebastian couldn't help but feel conflicted about the repercussions of what he just did. The good vibrations circulating his mind and body stemmed from knowing he protected someone who needed protecting. His actions saved Xavier from an episode of embarrassment. Sebastian could tell the team had used his new Asian buddy as their whipping boy before, but seeing it play out before his eyes made him want to put a stop to it. That meant shining a spotlight on himself even though a few hours ago no one cared to acknowledge him. Scoring three baskets against the heir apparent of the Cerano family all of sudden made the line to get info on Sebastian grow by the second, and Coach Barry Hankerson stood at the front of it. Similar to everyone else, a sense of curiosity drove the coach's interest in Sebastian.

Hankerson wanted to know more about Sebastian and passed his request for a meeting through Xavier. He didn't know what Sebastian would be walking into, but he did know he was called on to make that meeting happen. A tall order for the team manager who just met the kid everyone wanted get some info on.

"Coach would really like you to come to his office tomorrow morning before your first class. He rarely gets to school that early, so I'm sure he wants to tell you something pretty important. I mean he never comes in that early. And I know you just looked out for me but coach would look at me different if I was able to make this happen," Xavier explained.

"Why can't we talk now? I'm here now. Oh, I get it; coach doesn't want to seem like half these bitches in here waiting in line to ride my dick. Okay, you can tell him I'll see him in the morning. And tell him I want you to be there," Sebastian said.

"Me? Why me? You know I don't really have to come."

"Well, I think you should since Coach probably has something very important to tell me."
Xavier reluctantly agreed to show up for meeting and then ran off to tell Coach Hankerson the news.

Chapter 20

When Sebastian entered the gymnasium the next morning, he had no clue what he was walking into. He wondered if the embarrassment he caused Christian the day before would be responsible for exposing his secret. Xavier looked exhausted but was able to muster up a smile and head nod at his new buddy as they entered Coach Hankerson's office. Sebastian didn't get any warm looks from the coach, and his stoic look added to the tension-filled atmosphere. Although the coach's appearance left Sebastian with a bad taste in his mouth, he felt more comfortable once the meeting began.

"What you did to my star player may have been the best thing that could have happened to my team. These guys haven't had their shit together for a while. With three baskets against one guy you showed the entire team what I'd been saying to them since our season began. The reason I got my ass up at this godforsaken hour was to ask you if you would be interested in making a few more baskets as a member of this team," Coach Hankerson said.

Sebastian replied, "I love to play, but right now is not a good time for me to put basketball on my priority list. With school and..."

Coach Hankerson quickly interrupted when he realized Sebastian was about to take a pass on his offer. He countered Sebastian's argument by sweetening the deal. "I know school is important and that you may need some extra help with your studies. So I've already asked my cousin, Ms. Jordan, to give you some assistance with your

156

schoolwork. She's doing this as a favor for me, but she's on board."

Whatever thoughts Sebastian had about refusing Coach Hankerson's request were now extinct. He was looking for a way to get close to Ms. Jordan and now he had it.

"Okay, so where's my jersey?"

The Storm Raiders basketball program was well known in Ohio. Four state championship banners hung from the rafters in Sandusky Memorial's gymnasium. However, these just served as reminders of glory years gone by. The high school games were nothing more than a blip on the radar when it came to college scouts. Each year they had more wins than losses, but the Storm Raiders never made any major noise when the playoffs rolled around. Their last season of any significance was a distant memory. In recent years, much of the attention on high school basketball shifted east to Paul Brown Prep, a school in Cleveland where Cortez Buchanan played.

Cortez began taking the scholastic sports world by storm once he entered high school. His legend grew after and was featured on the cover of *Slam* magazine as a sophomore. The press branded him the second coming because of his nickname. He was labeled with the moniker Black Hova, which was a reference to his ethnicity and the Jehovah-like following spawned from the miracles he created on the court. People flocked to witness the skills on the court that mirrored the highlights of all the recent high school phenoms like LeBron James, Kobe Bryant, and Kevin Garnett. His acrobatics and smoothness on the court coupled with a forty-nine-game winning streak made the local and national press take notice of his limitless potential. His dominant play made him a can't-miss prospect, but his spectacular moves made his games must-see. Each time one of his plays was downloaded on YouTube, millions went to the site to check out Cortez's latest amazing move. He was a bona-fide national superstar as high school senior. Hoping to capitalize on Cortez's buzz the same way they did with LeBron James', ESPN set up a game to showcase the high school senior in front of a live audience. The sports television network opened a prime time slot to broadcast a game between America's number one high school basketball team Paul Brown Prep and the nationally ranked team—Kansas-based Winchester Prep. In the days leading up to the game, Cortez did several interviews to promote the game. The top ten plays of his short, but meteoric basketball career were plastered all over ESPN's website and television programming. The game was one day away when Mother Nature put the sports network's high school showcase in jeopardy of cancellation. There was a powerful tornado in Kansas, which was rare during autumn months. Even more of a rarity was the F-4 twister that touched down in the northern part of the state. The twister ripped through everything in its path including Winchester Prep and the homes of the players. The storm hit on the day the team was scheduled to depart for Cleveland, forcing ESPN to come up with a plan B. The goal was to create a match up that could generate a large TV audience. With Cortez being the only marquee name on the bill, the best game storyline ESPN producers could come up with and sell to advertisers was a David versus Goliath match-up. They had their Goliath, and a small list of Davids. Sandusky Memorial High School was at the top of it.

The Storm Raiders were going to be playing at a huge disadvantage, but Coach Hankerson was not a man who backed down from challenges. He immediately accepted the invitation when ESPN called. He couldn't hide his excitement when he started practice hours later. His team just set a date to meet up with a nationally ranked team on national television. The players were just as excited. Sebastian had a little bit of joy brewing inside him, but he had mixed feelings. He had just joined the team, and didn't know where he fit in. He also wondered if he could play and keep his hideout in Ohio a secret. Thoughts of the Capilini family learning of his whereabouts crept into his mind, but were quickly overshadowed by the competitive fire burning within him that hadn't been stoked since the game against the Russians. He didn't dwell on the dangers associated with playing for long. His new identity gave him a sense of security. Once he remembered he had a new name and a pretty good disguise going as a blond, his fears began to subside. Sebastian's love for basketball knew no boundaries, but once again that emotional attachment to the game was destined to put his life in danger.

Although he had convinced himself playing against Paul Brown Prep would be safe, he began to have second thoughts once he arrived home. Sebastian realized his survival wasn't just about him anymore.

"It looks like your settling fine. Now that you're on the team, this little set up looks like it's gonna work out after all," Gaucho said.

Sebastian wasn't used to being greeted with smiles and pleasantries when he walked through the front door. Over the weeks since his arrival, Gaucho had softened. Sebastian got the feeling the couple that took him in liked having him around. Betty was always breath of fresh air, and she would often let him know she loved having him around. Sebastian's transition to a small town teen was flowing smoothly, which is why he knew he had to lie about the game. He had no doubt Gaucho would never give the green light for him to play in a nationally televised game. It was the night before the biggest game of his life and Sebastian felt empty. He languished in guilt, knowing his actions were about to put Gaucho and Betty in danger. His concerns for the couple made him consider discussing the game as a family, but having a family talk at the kitchen table was abnormal behavior, Sebastian could not wrap his head around. Driven by his selfishness, Sebastian was not going to alter his plans. He decided silence and leaving a hand written note before departing for the team bus in the morning was the best route for him to take.

The atmosphere on the Storm Raiders bus was unlike any previous game. This was not a surprise to Coach Hankerson. He'd seen his players riled up before a playoff game, but their nervous demeanor before the biggest game of their lives needed to be shaken out of them. Coach Hankerson used some old school ways to apply a jolt to his rattled players. He boarded the bus with a bag filled with various colors of lipsticks. Each player looked perplexed as the coach walked through the bus handing out the make-up.

"I like my players to be prepared, and since all of you seem ready to line up with the rest of country to kiss the ass of the number one high school player in the country, why not add some color to your experience. You guys don't look like the Storm Raiders that I know. You look like a bunch of groupies ready to bend over like every piece of ass Cortez Buchanan has seen over the past year. I want winners on this bus. Do I have them? Do I have a group of guys ready to shock the world? Well, do I?" Coach Hankerson asked.

Sebastian looked around to see if any of his teammates were also finding it difficult to contain their laughter. No one shared his amusement. The coach's words were working. The team's competitive juices were flowing like a raging river. Coach Hankerson lead his players in the chant of "Ali Boom-Ba-Yay." Unfamiliar with the historic chant used by Muhammad Ali in Zaire before his fight with George Foreman, the team was slow to catch on. One by one they began to follow.

"Ali boom-ba-yay! Ali boom-ba-yay! Ali boom-ba-yay!"

The chorus of newly confident players chanted all the way to Quicken Loan arena in downtown Cleveland. The team's confidence was intact. They felt they could defeat whomever they met on the court. But, their confidence started to abate at the sight of the pristine hardwood, which was the home court of the Cleveland Cavaliers. This was by far the largest facility any of the Sandusky players had ever played in. This was also true for Sebastian, but the sense of excitement running through everyone's veins was not foreign to him. He'd gotten goose bumps in the same places before playing at Rucker Park against the city's best street ball players.

The Storm Raiders passed the players from Paul Brown Prep on their way to the locker room. Sebastian's teammates stared forward, but he made sure he locked eyes with Cortez Buchanan. It was his way of letting him know he was in for a long night.

The raucous crowd, bright lights, and television

cameras greeted each team once they exited their locker rooms and jogged onto the court. Sandusky started with their normal five players. From the tip off, Paul Brown Prep quickly reminded them why they were one of the top high school basketball teams in the nation.

Cortez knew the ESPN cameras were broadcasting his every move. Each time he got the ball, he made sure to put on a show. Every time his jump shot left his hand, the basketball found nothing but the bottom of the net. Each time Paul Brown Prep had a fast break, Cortez ended it with an explosive dunk. The game had all the signs of turning into the massacre the ESPN analysts predicted.

The Storm Raiders had their bright spots in the first five minutes of the game. Christian was playing his heart out, but with each passing minute he grew frustrated with his teammates. The courageous spirit they conjured up before the game had vanished, and Paul Brown Prep now lead Sandusky Memorial twenty-three to six after the first five minutes. That's when Sebastian made his move.

"Coach, I know every move that kid is about to make. I know I can shut him down, and when I do that, I know we can win," Sebastian said.

Coach Hankerson looked at his new recruit then looked at the other players on the bench. None of them mirrored the intensity Sebastian had in his eyes. He didn't know what Sebastian was capable of in a game situation, but Coach Hankerson was ready to find out.

Sebastian walked straight over to Cortez once he checked into the game. The two players were locked in an intense stare down. The television cameras immediately picked up on the adversarial vibe brewing. Sebastian wasn't intimidating his opponent one bit. Cortez understood he was being challenged and gladly accepted with a nod and a smile. Once the ref blew the whistle for the game clock to begin, Sebastian quickly showed Cortez what the rest of his night was going to be like. Cortez tried to use his crossover dribble to get past Sebastian.

"Get outta here with that bullshit!" Sebastian said. He quickly stripped the ball away and scored. The ESPN analyst and play-by-play commentator began to take note of Sebastian's performance. They were shocked watching every move made by the top high school player in the nation, countered by the new kid who just checked into the game. On defense, Sebastian turned Cortez's offensive skills into a non-factor. He could only score if he made it to the foul line. Other than that, the ESPN analysts were now talking about the handcuffs being applied to Cortez by Sebastian. On offense, the embarrassment continued. Sebastian put his team on his back, lifting them to a three point lead at half-time. In the second half, the embarrassment was taken up a notch. It was a moment no one saw coming. The ESPN commentators called the play the way everyone saw it.

"The Storm Raiders get a steal. It's a three-on-one fast break. Buchanan is known to be a great defender, but can he bust up the play? Cerano dishes to Caminzo. He takes off. Oh my! Oh my! Did he just jump over the number one high school player in the country? Who is this kid? Listen to this crowd!"

The dunk over Cortez sent the arena spectators into a frenzy. ESPN played the highlight several times. It took one play to make the aura around Cortez vanish. Meanwhile, Sebastian mesmerized the arena. His street ball moves left the opposing players looking for answers. They could not stop him from scoring. He made three-pointer after three-pointer. When he was finally double teamed, he passed the ball to an open teammate for an easy basket. With one minute left in the game, Sandusky Memorial High School was on the verge of writing their own version of David versus Goliath. The team needed one basket to kill Paul Brown Prep's chance of winning the game. Sebastian dribbled the ball at the top of the key until the twenty-second mark. His three-point shot hit nothing but net. The score was now fifty-seven to fifty.

Cortez tried to make a quick three-pointer to keep his team's chance of winning on life support, but the ball was stripped away by Sebastian, who had locked him up throughout the game. At the sound of the buzzer all of the Sandusky fans rushed the floor. Everyone was clamoring to hoist Sebastian onto his or her shoulders. As he was being carried to the locker room, Sebastian thought that for the first time his life was now heading in the direction he always wanted, and he didn't owe anyone a penny for it.

JAMAL A. BENJAMIN

Chapter 21

For most organized crime members high on the food chain, the weekends were meant for peace and quiet. Johnny Bats made a point to stay in New Jersey at his palatial home for that exact reason. Each Saturday morning he laid in his plush king size bed as long as possible. His two boys knew to keep the volume on the television and their discussions low. The ten and twelve-year-olds were avid basketball fans. They were too young to stay up to watch their favorite team, the Los Angeles Lakers, play on ESPN, so they made sure to watch the highlights first thing in the morning. Whatever they missed, they knew they could see on ESPN's *SportsCenter*. When the show came on, they were expecting to see the spectacular moves Kobe Bryant used to get the Lakers another win. Instead, the show began with a story about a little-known school named Sandusky Memorial High School and their huge upset win over Paul Brown Prep. The boys were glued to the television as they watched the magnificent moves performed by a high school player they'd never heard of.

Cortez Buchanan was well-known to the boys. They, like most basketball fans, believed he was the next LeBron James until he met Sebastian Caminzo. With each highlight, they could barely contain their excitement. Keeping quiet was becoming more and more difficult as replays of Sebastian's wizardry with the basketball played on the television screen. His high-flying dunk on Cortez's head made the boys break their silence.

"Oh!!!!!! He did not just dunk on him like that!" the

boys screamed.

Their yell was loud enough to be heard throughout the entire house and wake up their father. But they didn't care because they were too excited by the play and continued to celebrate it regardless of how enraged their awakened father would be. The celebration was cut short once their father came downstairs. Johnny smacked both of his sons in the back of the head and whipped out his belt.

"You two better have a good reason why you're howling like a pack of wolves so fucking early in the morning. What was so good about some fucking game that you had to act like you were in the goddamn arena? Now I wanna see this play, because just watching it is gonna give me more motivation to whip both of your asses," Johnny said.

His oldest son used TiVo to rewind the broadcast. Once the highlights started, Johnny couldn't take his eyes off the screen. From the moment he watched the kid his sons were yelling about, he wanted to kill him. He was no longer angry at being awakened. Johnny had murder on his mind because he recognized Sebastian Caminzo as the only person from BK To Tha Fullest his family hadn't killed. The lone survivor and his squad was responsible for costing the Capilini's millions of dollars. He now knew Barkley Capleton was alive and where to find him.

Detective Harrison had managed to keep himself under the radar of the Capilini family since he got his young friend out of town. They had no reason to suspect him of being the brains behind the plan that allowed Barkley to escape the violent end Kevlar, Moncrief, and his teammates met. Harrison was on his way to pick up his ten-year-old son when a familiar phone number rang his cell.

This was a phone call he didn't want to take and for good reason. Police work and playing the role of the Capilini family enforcer, kept him from spending quality time with his only son. There were times he was forced to abandon plans, leaving his little boy disappointed and drawing the ire of the child's mother. Harrison's ex-wife often denied his visitation rights thinking she was shielding their son from disappointment. It took some time, but Harrison's ex-wife began to notice his attempts to become a better father. He knew she reluctantly agreed to let their son stay with him for the weekend, so Harrison cleared his schedule to avoid any possible interruptions. When he picked up the call the voice on the other end was immediately recognized. Harrison previously heard that voice countless times, just never on his personal phone. The red flags in his mind immediately rose like the stars and stripes flapping in the wind at the library across the street. As he stood outside his ex-wife's door, he canvased the quiet suburban block to see if he was being watched. The neighborhood was safe, but as he cased his surroundings he was well aware that the Capilinis were no different from any other ruthless organized crime family, and regardless of the number of jobs he pulled for them, his paranoia made Harrison immediately feel he could be in real danger. He'd witnessed the family extend their hand to help one day, but follow up the good gesture with a double barreled shot gun to the face the next day, so anything abnormal about his dealings with the Capilinis made him nervous and in his mind, receiving a phone call from Arturo Capilini calling was very, very odd.

"My father wants you here now. We got a job for you and it needs to be handled ASAP."

"What the fuck is this? You know we have a systematic way of doing things. Bats is the only one I deal with. You know that," Harrison replied.

Arturo wasn't the sharpest knife in the drawer, so Harrison was surprised that Vincent Capilini even trusted his son with the easy job of setting up a meeting.

"I'm here and like he said we want you at our regular meeting spot now. See you in thirty," Johnny said.

"But I can't. This is my first weekend with my kid in months. We gotta reschedule."

"My father's here and he don't give a fuck. Get your ass here now!" Arturo yelled.

The call ended before Harrison could say anything more. He stood motionless wondering if he should try to explain the situation to his son or leave without indicating he showed up. The type of reception awaiting his arrival at the meet-up point with the Capilinis was an absolute mystery. They had plenty of reasons to take Harrison out if they worried about him turning into a witness for a federal prosecutor, but that was never really a concern because he had just as much to lose. Harrison never feared the Capilinis learning of his involvement in Barkley's relocation because it was a well-kept secret. He knew his son would be disappointed, but Harrison had to walk away. Brushing off a request from the head of the Capilinis was a treacherous road he did not want to head down. A disrespectful act of that magnitude would not only put a target on his back, but also put the lives of his ex-wife and child in jeopardy. His ex-wife and their son both watched from a second floor window, staring as Harrison made his painful exit. He sped off unsure of how his meeting with the Capilinis would play out. Several thoughts and scenarios consumed his mind, each one more violent than the next. Harrison even considered turning himself in and confessing to all the dirty work he amassed while working with the Capilinis. He came close to changing his destination to the NYPD headquarters at One Police Plaza, but fear took over. He feared what would happen to his son if he turned into a rat. Rolling the dice with his son's life was something Harrison would never do. In that moment he shut down his paranoia and continued on to the meet up location.

Three BMWs were parked outside the crime family-owned scrap yard in Newark. Harrison walked inside the office and saw Arturo, Vincent, Angelo, and Johnny sitting at a table. One of Arturo's two bodyguards walked toward Harrison and directed him to an empty chair at the table.

"Hey guys, do you wanna tell me why I had to rush over to this awkward ass meeting? I don't feel like sitting down. I just wanna know what this is all about, and I can get all of the details standing on my feet," Harrison said.

Vincent instructed Harrison to watch the flat screen television hanging on a nearby wall. An episode of ESPN *SportsCenter* was selected and played from the TiVo menu. The game footage initially pissed off Harrison. He wondered why the hell they called him in to talk about some player who didn't come through on a point shaving scam or some low life who's trying to skate on paying off a wager. Seconds later he understood why he was called in. Barkley's face was plastered all over each spectacular play highlighted on the show. He was even featured in the press conference following the game. His name was different. His hair color was different, but he looked exactly like the only member of BK To Tha Fullest who didn't make it to the morgue. There was no way in hell the Capilinis were not going to do something about that. Harrison had thoughts of pulling his gun and blasting his way out of there. He changed his mind when he realized they had no idea the role he played in saving the person they now knew as Sebastian Caminzo. Harrison understood he wouldn't have even made it to the meeting if his true role in the rescue plan were ever discovered.

"What the fuck am I watching here? Did you guys lose money on this game or some little shit like that? How the fuck is this my problem?" Harrison asked?

"We lost a lotta fuckin' money on some game, but it wasn't this one. The people responsible for that have been taken care of, except that back-stabbing nigger on the screen right there. I don't know how, but that street ballin' bastard got out of town and is breathing. We can't have that," Johnny said.

Harrison sat down at the table to listen to the Capilinis job offer. To his surprise they didn't want him to pull the trigger on this assignment. Arturo stated that the family hired a crew out of Chicago to carry out the execution of Barkley.

"I know you've done good clean-up work for us in the past, but you'd stick out like a rock hard dick if we sent you there to take out Barkley, I mean Sebastian, or whatever the fuck his name is. We want this done clean, and we need some locals or a crew familiar with that area, to handle this," Vincent said.

Harrison was going to play bagman on this job. Once the job was done, he would hand over the bag holding one hundred thousand dollars to the contracted killers before they headed back to Chicago. Along with learning the details of the kill contract, Harrison found out that the hired killers were brothers who had done previous work for the family. They were meticulous and performed research before executing their targets. The Krakowski brothers were already on the road to Sandusky with orders to have Barkley on a city morgue slab in forty-eight hours.

The Capilinis booked a flight for Harrison to get to Cleveland the next day. From there he would drive to Sandusky to meet up with the Krakowski brothers to hand over the money. He wasn't given a photo of the kill team, only a cell phone that would ring once the job was done. They would provide instructions of the drop point and part ways after the money was exchanged. The job would have been the simplest task ever given to Harrison by the Capilinis, however that was not the case in this situation. He left the scrap yard office with a huge dilemma drilling a Texas-size hole in his head. Driving with the money to finance the murder of his friend, Harrison felt an enormous weight on his shoulders. The rescue plan he designed was about to be dismantled by professional killers and he felt it was his responsibility to stop them. Harrison didn't have time to wait for a flight. Once he hopped on the road, he was headed toward Sandusky. It was a long ten-hour drive, but a short time to figure out how he was going to keep himself alive and save the people he'd rescued once before.

JAMAL A. BENJAMIN

Chapter 22

Detective Harrison had managed to walk a tightrope during his long career in the NYPD. Although he took the lives of several people at the request of the Capilinis, he gained a reputation of being a good cop. He scraped the scum off city streets with intelligence and hard-nosed police work. Each case that landed on his desk, he closed by the book. He occasionally used some muscle to get a confession, but outside of smacking around guilty criminals the tactics used to get a conviction were rarely questionable. He knew his current task was going to call for him to get dirty and use all of the underworld intelligence he acquired over the years. Outsmarting trained killers and manipulating a crime family bent on revenge was the only way Harrison was going to walk away unscathed and with all of his friends alive. Several scenarios played out in his head as he drove on Interstate 80 towards Ohio. Making a phone call to get his friends out of the scope of the Capilini family would be easy enough, but even at a time of dire circumstance, self-preservation was his primary focus. If Barkley pulled a disappearing act, a firing squad would definitely be dispatched to carry out the Capilini's vengeance on Harrison. He then thought he could call Gaucho to give him a heads up. The phone rang once before he hung up. He remembered how easily rattled Gaucho could become and a phone call would definitely make him panic. What Harrison had to say, needed to be said in person. Even if Harrison's call had gotten through to warn of the death squad heading toward Sandusky, it would have gone unanswered. There was a huge victory party going on in the small town and everyone was celebrating as if they'd just won the Super Bowl.

Barkley Capleton was marked for death, but the violent retribution in store for him was the furthest thing from his mind. He had been reborn as Sebastian Caminzo and everyone loved him for putting their town on top of the sports world. ESPN, television news crews from Cleveland and Toledo, plus sportswriters from the nation's top sports publications converged on the campus of Sandusky Memorial High School to get the scoop on the kid who led his team to victory. The team was surprised with a pep rally that was attended by almost the entire town when they returned home two days after their upset win. Queen's "We Are The Champions" blared from the school's marching band's horn and percussions section as they escorted the team bus down the street. The parade procession traveled five miles along Patriot Road toward the front entrance of the high school. The players immediately became excited at the sight of their school adorned in decorations and surrounded by screaming supporters. Sebastian had just been there a short time, but he felt the love. As each player's name was announced, that person got off the bus and ran up to the pep rally stage. Three players had exited when Sebastian was making his way off the bus. Before his name could be called, Coach Hankerson stopped him.

"You wait right here for a second. You guys go ahead. I think the announcement of our new co-captain needs to be something we need to build a little anticipation for don't you?" Coach Hankerson asked.

Sebastian was the last player announced, but the crowd made him feel like he was first in their hearts. He received the loudest applause out of all the players. Photographers showered him with flashes as they took his photo. Among the many photographers were two men who had traveled from Chicago. They snapped several photographs. They even snapped photos of the guy Sebastian attempted to call up on stage. Overcome with nervousness, Sebastian stopped at the base of the stage staircase. He reached out for the only person who had helped him thus far. The enormous expression of gratitude was overwhelming and he needed help dealing with it. Gaucho declined the offer. He was smiling like the rest of the crowd, but the fugitive from Capilini justice knew deep inside this situation was going to put a spotlight on the hideout he'd been holed up in for the last ten years. There were a few folks in the crowd attempting to nudge him up to the stage. The nudges from a few spectators, coupled with Sebastian's insistence, made the Krakowski brothers Victor and Aidan turn their camera lens toward Gaucho. As Victor snapped photos, his younger brother Aidan headed back to their van to email the photos to the Capilini family. He sent each photo they snapped of Barkley plus the ones of the man he requested on stage.

It was only a matter of time before Gaucho's decade-long vanishing act would be exposed.

JAMAL A. BENJAMIN

Chapter 23

At the end of the pep rally, everyone wanted to get up close and personal with Sebastian. Each time he turned to walk in any direction, he was met by one of his new fans. The barrage of attention was beginning to suffocate Sandusky Memorial's new Mr. Popular. He felt as if he was in a spin cycle before Gaucho reached in to grab him.

"Hey folks, he's not going anywhere and he's had a long day so we're gonna head home," Gaucho said.

With his arm wrapped around Sebastian, Gaucho walked him out of the jaws of the frenzied crowd. They walked past several well-wishers before coming to their first member of the press.

"I write for the *Toledo Telegraph*. Your story is very remarkable and I think people should hear about it. Here's my card. Please give me a call," Victor said.

He was dressed for the part and played it well. Neither Gaucho nor Sebastian was suspicious of Victor Krakowski playing the role of a newspaper sports reporter. Gaucho took the card, and continued leading Sebastian out of the maze of supporters and members of the press. There were interview requests from *Sports Illustrated*, ESPN, Comcast Sports, local newspaper writers, and television reporters. They all wanted to know about the kid who crushed the baddest high school baller in the country. The attention was overwhelming for Sebastian, but he still felt an inner urge to indulge in the celebrity his accomplishment was creating. There was something inside him that made him wonder if this was an opportunity he should capitalize on.

All of the attention was entirely too much for Gaucho. His relaxed and low-key life was being rattled by a media firestorm that threatened to destroy everything he had created. His connection to Sebastian made life dangerous for Gaucho and he was very vocal about that when they arrived at his car.

"I should fuck you up for that bullshit note you left to begin with, but you wouldn't give a fuck about what you did anyway. I've managed to stay alive the only way I can. It's the only way anyone who has chosen this life manages to stay alive. You go underground and you stay there. My world has been quiet and complete since escaping from New York. Now, in less than a month you're about to reduce it to fucking rubble."

Sebastian could care less about what Gaucho was saying. His mind had already begun to wander. Gaucho continued his tirade, but the volume of his voice was soon drowned out by the basketball fantasies stirring in Sebastian's swelled head. Once he realized his words of wisdom were falling on deaf ears, rage erupted from inside Gaucho. That was the last straw for him. He jumped out of the car.

"Get the fuck out of my car. I'm not gonna let you fuck up my life. I'm not gonna let you hang a death sentence over my head," Gaucho said.

Sebastian sat in the car refusing to leave. He heard the demands for his exit, but he knew he couldn't leave at that time. In between the praises from the folks in town and the sexual advances from cheerleaders, Coach Hankerson had told him four college coaches already reached out to get information on the kid who slayed a basketball giant. They all wanted to know about Sebastian Caminzo. After hearing that, Sebastian knew he had to take advantage of the opportunity he created for himself on the basketball court in Cleveland. It was his only way to change his destiny.

Gaucho grew louder and louder with his demands. He only stopped when his lady pulled up to meet them at the school parking lot. Betty had never seen her man that angry and wanted to know what made him that way. Still living a lie of his own, Gaucho calmed down to let his lady know it was nothing more than just a difference of opinion between he and his nephew. Similar to previous times when there seemed to be more to what her man was telling her, she took his word for it and dropped the issue. Her mind shifted to the real reason she left her shop to find Gaucho. Coach Hankerson left a voice mail on the house phone about an interview request made by ESPN. Betty couldn't stop smiling as she recited what she had heard. Big time sports cameras, and television crews were in her town and would soon be at her door-step. Without saying a word, Gaucho walked backed to the car and sat behind the wheel.

"Thank you for the news, Betty," Sebastian said.

Gaucho drove off and Betty followed. They all went home, unaware that the entire incident played out before the eyes of Victor as he watched from behind a nearby tree.

Sandusky didn't have many hotels to choose from. The town's premier hotels were palatial and provided a comforting atmosphere. They were just what the visiting press ordered when it came to accommodations. For the Krakowski brothers, those kind of dwellings made it harder for the job they came there to do. The professional hit men set up shop at a roadside motel just outside Sandusky. Aidan had just finished setting up their room when his brother arrived from doing his mission research. Each brother's .45 semi-automatic pistol lay on the bed beside an AR-15 with a silencer and scope. Before his brother walked in, Aidan had just finished using a laptop and scanner to send their remaining photos to the Capilini family. Before killing anyone the brothers would always email photos of each person they were hired to kill to confirm they had the right person(s). They usually received immediate confirmation through a text message. Twenty minutes had passed without a response. The brothers began to discuss shutting down the operation if they didn't hear anything in the next five minutes. The cancellation discussion ended when Aidan's phone rang. It was Arturo. His orders were simple.

"We want everyone dead. We want that fucking kid dead. We want that guy with him dead. We want anyone living with that guy dead. We want the bagman with your money dead."

"That's gonna cost you a lot more than one hundred grand," Aidan said.

"We've already put a guy on a plane to take care of you guys. An extra one hundred and fifty grand is heading your way. It arrives in Cleveland tomorrow night. It'll be there for you after you take out the bagman you're supposed to meet up with."

"We don't work like this. Does your father know you're changing up the order?"

"What's with all the fucking questions? Take the job, or we'll have someone else do it."

The rage in Arturo's voice wasn't a clear indicator, but he had been shaken by the photos he received. This was the first time he'd made the brazen move to change the details attached to a kill order. Aidan told him he would need a few minutes to talk it over with his brother.

For Arturo that three-minute wait seemed like an eternity. With each passing second, he was reminded the one person who knew his dark secret was still walking the earth. He conjured up ill-fated scenarios that ended with disgrace to his father and his own death. His blood pressure lowered once Aidan called him back to accept his new order. The body count on this mission went from one to four, but the brothers did not want to make their job any more bloody or noisy than it had to be. In order to do that, they put Betty first on their kill list. They had no clue where their main target was residing, but they did know where they could find Betty. Her shop's bright logo on her car led them straight to her.

JAMAL A. BENJAMIN

Chapter 24

A beam of sunlight shined brightly through Sebastian's bedroom window the next morning. He lied in his bed, gazing at the honey-coated hue draped over the bedroom doorway. He slept on and off through the night. Fragments of his conversation with Gaucho pierced the center of his mind, but it was the words of Coach Hankerson that turned his mind into a fantasy factory. His imagination churned out several scenarios where all of his hoop dreams came true. Much of the excitement in his brain was over his highly anticipated meeting with the coach that morning. They were going to discuss the multiple requests coming from college coaches to meet up with him. With his heated argument with Gaucho still producing a high level of tension, Sebastian got dressed and exited the house without crossing paths with Betty or Gaucho. When he arrived for his 8 a.m. meeting, Sebastian joined the small group of students waiting in front of the school to be let in for first period. His brain was wrapped around another one of his fantasies when he felt a tap on his shoulder and a familiar voice.

"You know, the way you play reminds of me of this kid named Barkley. You know him?" Harrison said.

Time froze momentarily for Sebastian. He recognized the voice, but he didn't want to think about what that meant. The few words uttered by Harrison quickly reminded Sebastian of where he was, and why he was there, and that scared him. Turning around to see the man responsible for saving his life would have been a cause for celebration a week ago, but he knew Harrison was not in town because he missed him. They shook hands, embraced, and exchanged a few pleasantries. The cordial behavior came to an end once the conversation was moved to the adjacent teachers' parking, which was a secluded area where they could speak freely.

"I can't say this any more clearly than what I'm about to say. You gotta get the fuck outta here. Not later today, not tomorrow, but right fucking now," Harrison said.

Sebastian's reaction to Harrison's words mirrored his response to Gaucho's comments. Sensing his heartfelt remarks were falling on deaf ears, Harrison resorted to a tactic he often used in his interrogations. Sebastian's feet briefly left the ground when Harrison's hand came across his face. Stumbling into a nearby fence kept him from hitting the ground. He barely got to his feet before Harrison jumped on him again. The forceful blow levied a shock to Sebastian's system, dazing the teen until he received his next jolt of reality. Harrison grabbed him and pushed him into the gate by his collar.

"You don't know how many lives are at stake! How many can get killed, and you're on top of the fucking list. That was a great show you put on the other night; too bad you won't get a chance for an encore since the Capilinis sent a kill squad to put your ass in the ground with the rest of your old teammates."

"What the fuck you want me to do? That train has left the fucking station and if you think I wanna live off the tracks like your boy Gaucho, I'd rather live the little bit of life I have left," Sebastian responded.

"What the fuck is this poetic shit? Listen to me now and listen to me good. You need to get ghost real fast. Get the fuck outta this town and save some lives in the process, one of them being your own."

"And what happens then—I keep hiding out and you go back to your fucking life of playing good cop, bad cop right?"

Hearing those comments made Harrison soften his grip on Sebastian. For the very first time in their relationship, Sebastian was going to be the one delivering the straight talk. Filled with emotions, his eyes began to water. Sebastian's heartfelt words reminded Harrison what happened the last time Sebastian had an emotional breakdown. They were a long way from Coney Island, so instead of telling Sebastian to shout out his demons, he decided to listen. This was the first time Harrison learned how basketball became Sebastian's savior long before he came in the picture. Balling on the blacktop helped him drown out the memories of a mother who abandoned him. He detailed how the joys associated with hitting a jump shot from every inch of the court picked him up when he contemplated suicide after one of Mother Benson's boyfriends sexually abused him. At the age of ten he was forced to stroke the monster's penis each time she was passed out drunk. That year long abuse would have continued, but she kicked him to the curb after she grew tired of his inability to keep his dick hard long enough for her to sit her grotesque ass on it. His story also included times when he bared witness to atrocities.

Living life as Barkley Capleton was no easy task. He understood he was only alive because of a few special guardian angels, and recognized one of them was standing right in front of him. Sebastian was thankful for what Harrison had done to save his life, but that didn't mean the cop owned him. He made it clear, his gratitude did not mean he was relinquishing control of his life. With confidence in his voice, Sebastian told him he was taking on the role of director in this second act of his life, and although he initially made the transition to Sebastian kicking and screaming, he was now adjusting to living a new life. A new life he didn't want give up. A new life that made him courageous enough to question his protector.

"Why is it everyone but you always has to change? Gaucho has to leave his life and lose a finger because you don't wanna do the right thing," Sebastian said.

Harrison was beginning to grow agitated. He dipped into his pocket for a cigarette to calm himself down, but Sebastian's fuse had already been lit. He wanted answers to his questions.

"You got enough evidence to shut down the Capilinis and make their asses extinct, but you'd also have to shit on yourself. And Detective Harrison can't handle the stench connected to what he's done, can he?"

"You got all the answers, kid, don't you?"

He was moving in closer to give Sebastian an earful, when Coach Hankerson interrupted his oncoming tirade.

"Hey, Sebastian, are we meeting about these college offers or what?" Coach Hankerson shouted.

"Yeah, I'm coming. I got nothing to lose," Sebastian replied as he turned his back on Harrison and walked away.

With a life-changing moment within his grasp, Sebastian's mind could not conjure up any delusions of grandeur. It was clouded by the recent implosion of a friendship that saved his life on more than one occasion.

His face mirrored a blank slate as he stepped into Coach Hankerson's office.

"You've either just seen a ghost or you just lost someone really close to you," Coach Hankerson said.

"Is it possible both can happen at the same time?" Sebastian asked.

The bizarre question puzzled the coach, but he was too excited about the good news he wanted to share, to dissect his star player's comment. Coaches from Division 1 basketball programs at Kentucky, Cincinnati, Penn State, Ohio State, and Marquette were headed to Sandusky to watch Sebastian play in Memorial High's next game. Syracuse, Georgetown, Virginia Tech, and Duke RSVP'd for the following game. The excitement oozed from every pore on Coach Hankerson's body, but Sebastian could barely move a facial muscle to make a smile. Coach Hankerson's rising voice and celebratory tone did nothing to lift Sebastian out of his funk.

"Kid, I'm pulling for you, but you gotta tell me what's going on with you. Yesterday you're on top of the world. Today it's like you just came from a funeral."

The coach's pleas for feedback were interrupted by a knock at the door. It was the one person who could get Sebastian's attention at that moment. Her request to enter immediately removed the tension from the room.

"Hey guys, I knew you were meeting so I thought we could possibly confirm a time to meet up with the town's newest celebrity before his scheduled filled up," said Ms. Jordan.

Ms. Jordan's arrival immediately jarred Sebastian from his trance. He twisted his body nearly 180° to look at her.

"Hi, Sebastian. Do you have a little time you can spend with me?" Ms. Jordan asked with a smile.

"I don't know, cousin, this kid is not translating the English language very well this morning. I just told him he's got a full scholarship being offered by some of the best schools in the country and he went mute on me," Coach Hankerson said.

The coach's words angered Sebastian for a brief moment. He didn't take too kindly to the embarrassing comments, but he quickly returned his attention to Ms. Jordan.

"I think it'd be perfect if we drove to my uncle's house after school, say 4 p.m." Sebastian said.

"Wow! He speaks," Coach Hankerson said.

It was clear Sebastian was smitten with his teacher. He shed his hardened exterior for the moment and smiled when Ms. Jordan agreed to the time set by Sebastian. She exchanged a few words with her cousin, then left a stern warning with Sebastian before departing.

"I'm not doing this get in good with a future NBA star. I'm doing this because I care about education. Do not waste my time, and if you think I'm gonna let you quit, you got a big problem on your hands."

Her exit made Sebastian's heart beat at a faster rate than it did when she made her entrance. Now that he was awakened and freed from his frozen state, Coach Hankerson continued to lay out the details of the treasure trove of opportunities being laid at his feet. The pair hammered out a simple plan to get him the full scholarship best fit for his game and personality. For the next two games, the team's offense was going to run through Sebastian, giving him the green light to take as many shots as he wanted. The coach wasn't much of a motivational speaker, but Sebastian understood that this would be the most pressure-filled situation he ever had to endure. In Sebastian's mind, it wasn't insurmountable. These next two games were all that was needed to get him to the level where he had always dreamed of playing.

Across town there was another important discussion taking place, though this one was more sinister. The type of weapons the Krakowski brothers used all depended on the type of job they were doing. Now that the body count was going to be north of what they originally planned, they opted for weapons that would allow them to get up close before blowing their target's brains out. The brothers cleaned every inch of their sleek nickel-plated .45 caliber cannons, which sparkled in the sunlight that shined through their motel room window. The silence in the room was broken by Victor's request for Aidan to run through the order of events scheduled for the day. Before Aidan could begin, Victor told him to include the times they scheduled for each action. Clearly agitated by his brother's attention to detail, Aidan began the rundown.

At 3 p.m. Victor was going to place a call to Betty at her store to inform her that there's been an accident and she has to get home right away. She would be told she needs to convince Gaucho to go to the hospital after a fall down the stairs. When she speeds off in her car to head home, the Krakowski brothers planned to be right behind her. At 3:15 p.m. they would be in place to intercept her car five miles before she arrives home. From there, she'd be forced to drive both assassins to her home. At 3:30 p.m. both brothers would walk Betty inside. They expected to be confronted by Gaucho who would be kept at bay by the sight of a gun being placed at the head of the most important person in his life. After he is instructed to call Sebastian home, Victor would instruct Aidan to shoot him in the head. Seconds later, Betty's life would be taken in the same fashion by Victor. At 3:45 p.m. the bodies would be placed in the basement. At 4 p.m. Sebastian would walk in the home and be killed two minutes after closing the door. Gaucho's car would be used as the escape vehicle to return to their car. At 4:15 p.m. they would depart for Cleveland to execute the final portion of their contract with the Capilinis.

"Well done, little brother," Victor said.

Chapter 25

The bottle was always Detective Harrison's sanctuary when tough times came knocking at his door. His blow up with Sebastian was just the latest reason he invited Jack Daniels into his life. The flask with his initials was no longer giving him enough liquid courage, so he started taking swigs straight from the bottle. The whiskey worked well to drown the anguish he was experiencing over the heated exchange with Sebastian. He couldn't just cut ties with the kid he spent years protecting. Each time he took it to the head he envisioned a bloody end to Barkley's life. Looking the other way was becoming harder and harder by the minute. The Capilini wolves were circling and Harrison had a short amount of time to figure out a rescue plan. He thought of several scenarios, but none included sacrificing himself. The whiskey was destroying his brain cells at a rapid rate and ushered him into an unconscious state. Like many times before, Harrison drank away his sorrow for the time being. His sleep swept his cowardly feelings, but in the process stripped him of valuable planning time.

Hours had passed When Harrison finally opened his eyes it was mid-afternoon. The digital clock on his motel room dresser flashed noon, but Harrison's gut told him that part of the day had passed some time ago. His hangover made it difficult to find his phone, but then he remembered he placed it inside his jacket. The clock on his iPhone read 2:45 p.m. His brain almost immediately began operating in the same fashion it did before the whiskey knocked him out. Thinking only made his brain feel like it was wrapped in barb wire. His planning was nowhere near the starting gate. Four doors down the hallway at the same motel, the Krakowski brothers' plan was right on schedule. Both dressed in attire that made them look like unassuming golfers, hiding their true identities. The polo shirts and khaki pants made them look like anything but the killers they were planning on becoming in a short period of time. The brothers completed their transformation into killing machines by loading their .45 caliber pistols, and screwing the silencers on the barrel. As they walked to their car, the brothers heard Harrison's frustration boil over. The crashing sound of the Jack Daniels bottle smashing against a wall stopped them in their tracks. They stood outside the room of the man they were hired to kill, but continued on their mission unaware of his close proximity. Harrison collapsed to his knees cursing his friend for making his life so difficult. It was clear he couldn't let Sebastian die. His outburst of anger cleared his mind, which ushered in an idea he hadn't considered before. He realized Gaucho wanted Sebastian out of town just as much as he did. Gaucho didn't want Sebastian in his home to begin with. Harrison would be doing Gaucho a favor by taking Sebastian off his hands and he was sure Gaucho would help. It was a plan that required some muscle and rough housing, but it was all he could come up with. Harrison hopped in his car and headed to Gaucho's house to get his old friend to partner up with him on his new plan.

Since Sebastian's game in Cleveland, Gaucho hadn't experienced very many peaceful afternoons. His home phone rang continuously every day and each time he picked up, it was some journalist or TV reporter soliciting him for access to Sebastian. The interview requests reached fifty before he decided it was best to take the phone off the hook. He could care less about giving Sebastian exposure. In his mind, he was already in danger and living on borrowed time. It wasn't his photo plastered on ESPN.com, newspapers, or basketball magazines, but he thought in some strange way his quiet life in Ohio was about to get loud in very bad way. In years past, Gaucho would have hit the road. He'd done it before. When an inner voice told him he wasn't safe, his skill of vanishing without a trace was put into practice. This time things were different. Falling in love with Betty erased his ability to pull a disappearing act. Leaving the woman he loved was not an option he was ready to entertain. He wondered if Sebastian's new popularity was putting her life in danger. In that instance, he thought to check up on her. It was 3:15 p.m. when he decided to call. His first call went unanswered. It was odd for Betty to miss a call from Gaucho. It had happened before and she would call back, but on this occasion Gaucho immediately called back to see if he received the same result. The second call ended like the first. There was no answer on the other end, but Gaucho was not alarmed by the missed call. He was confident she would return his call very soon. Unbeknownst to him, his lady was becoming the first cog in the Krakowskis' wheel of mob justice.

Betty quickly surrendered to the Krakowski brothers' aggressive driving tactics. They rammed the rear of her car continuously until she tail-spinned off the road. Her car came to a rest at the bottom of an embankment. She was conscious, but dazed and clueless as to why she'd become a victim of road rage. Her assailants were kind as they helped her out of the car, but that was a short-lived gesture. They wanted to know where she lived, and they weren't nice about it. She was stood up against her car for interrogation. Due to her frazzled state, most of the their questions went unanswered. Simple questions about Sebastian's whereabouts and who was currently residing at the home were met with silence.

Vincent asked the questions while Aidan sifted through Betty's car for her purse. They wanted to know where she lived, but her state of shock was becoming a major disruption in their timetable. Thinking a little jolt would jar her memory, Vincent began trying to shake the information out of her. His rage grew with each passing second Betty continued to be non-responsive. He raised his hand to smack her, but Aidan's discovery of her purse stopped the hostage situation from becoming violent for the time being. The Krakowski brothers were a step closer to honoring their contract with the Capilinis. Before moving forward, they had a decision to make. The crash left Betty's car a wreck. This forced the brothers to change their plan. They were now going to have to drive their car to the house where two of their targets would be. The decision to end Betty's life had already been made, but they had to determine whether it would be best to carry it out in the wooded area. Eventually they decided it would be best to put Betty in the trunk of their car for now and kill her later. The brothers loaded her in and headed off to bring a close to the lives of Sebastian and Gaucho.

The signs of the day coming to an end were beginning to show when Sebastian and Ms. Jordan arrived at his house in her 1998 Honda Accord. Gaucho saw them and immediately became uncomfortable and agitated. It served as a reminder he was no longer going to be able to live the secluded life he enjoyed.

The ride from school was an entertaining one for Sebastian and Ms. Jordan. They talked basketball, but Sebastian was more interested in how he could get her to see him in a romantic way. Although they'd arrived, Sebastian bombarded with Ms. Jordan with questions he knew she wouldn't answer in the presence of others. His charm made her lower her guard enough to reveal some scintillating details about her private life. Sebastian learned Ms. Jordan hadn't been on a good date in over six months. She occasionally spoke with a college sweetheart who she almost married. She'd even traveled to Cleveland to meet him for dinner and a fun-filled weekend. He didn't say it, but Sebastian could clearly tell she was still getting dick from her ex. She was also a couple years older than her ex, so that inspired Sebastian to hope Ms. Jordan was still interested in younger men. His ability to keep her laughing also served as a beacon of hope in his quest to win her heart.

Sebastian was careful not to say anything that would cause a red flag to go up when the conversation shifted to his background. There were so many lies stored in his head that he didn't know which ones to go with. His goal of becoming her lover swayed him away from making up stories about being abandoned. Instead he fabricated a story that would make him look more macho.

"My uncle brought me out here because I was taking care of myself after my mother suffered from mental health issues. Her schizophrenia became too overwhelming and she was committed," Sebastian said.

He immediately felt her marvel at his resilience. In that short amount of time, Sebastian felt a bond developing. His master plan was working. It was working so well, she didn't flinch as he grabbed her hand when they shared a laugh. Sebastian attempted to keep the conversation moving, but Ms. Jordan stopped him in his tracks.

"This has been one of the better conversations I've had in a while but we got to get going on your school work before it gets too late. But this is something we can definitely revisit," Ms. Jordan said. Sebastian agreed to bring the conversation to a close but only if Ms. Jordan agreed to stay for dinner. "You're definitely going to be a problem. I can see that now. If that'll get you to open your books, then fine, yes, I'll stay for dinner."

As the two of them walked to the house, Sebastian couldn't help but feel good about the progress he was making in the pursuit of his teacher. That was until he turned his head to look behind himself and saw a familiar car heading his way. Harrison was speeding toward the house, and Sebastian knew there wasn't going to be anything rosy about another reunion. His anxiety was rooted in his recollection of their last encounter. Sebastian ushered Ms. Jordan into the house to remove her from witnessing any drama. His reprieve from conflict was short lived. Ms. Jordan's scream was a clear indicator of this. As soon as they entered the home, Gaucho was standing there with his rifle in his hand.

"What the fuck is this, man?" Sebastian asked.

He stepped in front of Ms. Jordan to shield her from any violence.

"I want my life back. Ever since you came here, my life has been turned upside down. I've survived doing things a certain way. And you're fucking with that," Gaucho said.

If the conditions were fair, Sebastian would have

stood the best chance of coming out the victor. He was taller, younger, more agile, and more than strong enough to take Gaucho off his feet with one punch. However, Gaucho was drunk and holding a rifle in his palms with enough firepower to end Sebastian's life with one shot.

Gaucho moved forward, forcing Sebastian and Ms. Jordan to back out of the house. This was not the situation Harrison envisioned when he pulled up to Gaucho's home. He had intended on carrying Sebastian out of town if he had to, but he definitely did not want it to be in a body bag. Instead of enforcer, Harrison entered the situation as a peacemaker.

"Whoa, whoa, old buddy. There's no need to put a hole in any one. You and I want the same thing. We both want this naive fucker out of your life. So let's make that happen without the gun," Harrison said.

His words helped Gaucho settle down. It wasn't enough to make him loosen his grip on his rifle, but they did make him feel comfortable about lowering his gun. The tension was still at a suffocating level. Ms. Jordan was trembling. Sebastian felt the vibration of her body on his back. He knew he had gotten her into a situation that was caused by his own doing. The body count connected to Sebastian since the game with the Russians was already high and he didn't want it rising at the expense of Ms. Jordan's life.

"Okay, okay, I know what I have to do. If that means me leaving, then so be it, but I don't want anyone to get hurt. That's a sacrifice, and I'm willing to sacrifice so others don't get killed. Isn't that what I should do Detective Harrison?" Sebastian asked in a condescending tone.

He wrapped his arms around Ms. Jordan to walk her

to her car. His motion made Gaucho and Harrison a little edgy, but he calmed them down and promised he wouldn't try to make an escape. She was a nervous wreck, which made walking difficult. Sebastian kept her upright and she held on tight. As they walked toward her car, Ms. Jordan pulled Sebastian closer so he could hear the comments she whispered.

"I can't leave you here. When we get to my car I want you to hop in and we'll both get the hell out of here."

Her words touched his heart. It was the first time someone made him feel like his life was more important than theirs. Although the words gave Sebastian a heavy heart, he ignored Ms. Jordan's pleas. There were two men behind them who could potentially get violent. He reconsidered making a run for it with Ms. Jordan after spotting a blue Chevrolet Caprice heading their way up the long driveway, but Sebastian did not recognize the car. Neither did anyone else, but Aidan and Victor recognized everyone except for Ms. Jordan,, and planned to deal her a fate they were contracted to hand each of their original targets. Everyone's anxiety level went up a few notches when Gaucho told Harrison he wasn't expecting any visitors. As the car pulled in, Gaucho recognized the driver. He recalled his conversation with the driver, who'd earlier identified himself as a reporter with the *Toledo Telegraph*, but this time, he was not there to ask any questions. Gaucho had grown irritated by all members of the media with their non-stop calling and request for interviews. With a gun in his hand, he couldn't think of a better way of telling the man he thought was a reporter, how he really felt about his interview request. He walked toward the car with his rifle aimed Victor and Aidan, who had just exited their car.

199

"I'm gonna need you to get the fuck off my property and go back to where you came from. If you wanna live to tell another motherfucking story, make a U-turn now!" Gaucho said.

Both brothers kept their poise as they stood in at the end of Gaucho's rifle. Each had their own arsenal within arms reach on their waist. The Krakowskis liked to keep their work clean. They were capable of unleashing a barrage of bullets that would have killed everyone in front of them, but there was nothing about a shootout in northern Ohio that translated into a good business move.

"Sir, if you want us to leave we will. I just don't feel good about getting in my car staring down the barrel of a loaded gun," said Victor.

Aidan knew what his brother was setting up. All they needed was a small window to execute their plan, and getting Gaucho to lower his gun was going to give them a big enough gap to start their killing spree. Victor continued offering words to comfort Gaucho. Unaware the men standing before him were hired killers with a contract to execute everyone including himself, Harrison began to utter words that could peacefully end the ordeal.

"Lower the gun and let these guys go. They're just here to do a job," Harrison said.

Although he offered a peaceful resolution, Harrison's comments escalated the situation. The Krakowski brothers recognized him. The siblings quickly glanced at each other to make sure they were on the same page. In that instance the plan to kill Harrison in Cleveland was now scrapped. They now intended to kill everyone standing in front of them. Gaucho listened to Harrison's attempt to broker a non-violent resolution. He agreed to lower his gun but only when both men returned to their car. The situation was playing out just as the Krakowski brothers wanted it to. They were just seconds away from showering each target with gunfire when a female voice could be heard making pleas for assistance.

"Help!!!"

The shrieking voice hollered help again and again. Betty's voice was not initially recognized, but her calls for help did not fall on deaf ears.

"What the fuck is that? Who the fuck is that?" Gaucho said.

"Clarence, is that you? Please do what they want and help me," Betty continued.

The Krakowski brothers briefly locked eyes with Gaucho before they pulled out their guns and began to fire. The first barrage of bullets hit Gaucho in the leg. He was falling to the ground but managed to get off a shot. He did not aim well, but his first and only shot found its mark. It was Victor Krakowski's head. The bullet traveled thought his skull before exiting the back of his head. Victor was instantly killed. Aidan fired in the direction of the three remaining targets. Sebastian and Ms. Jordan ran for the house. She held his hand tight to keep up with Sebastian's dash for the house. He felt her firm grip up until they were steps away from the front entrance. Her body fell to the ground lifeless. Sebastian thought Ms. Jordan tripped, but when he turned around, he quickly learned something more disastrous had occurred. Bullets whizzed by him as he crawled toward her. He managed to get to her without taking a bullet, but once he turned her over, the pain he felt was greater than any bullet wound he could have suffered. Her angelic face was scratched up from the fall and her body leaked blood from the bullet hole in her chest. Aidan had both in his sights ready to fire when he noticed his brother was no longer standing on the other side of the car. His call for Victor went unanswered. He quickly canvassed the area and discovered he was the last man standing. Harrison laid on the ground the motionless. Sebastian was holding Ms. Jordan rocking back and forth hoping his words could magically bring her back to life. Aidan directed his attention to the last location he saw his brother. It only took him three footsteps to learn why Victor was not standing beside him—he saw his brother's lifeless body was stretched out toward the back of the car. Aiden briefly stared at his brother before pointing his gun at Gaucho. The bullet in his leg made an escape from death impossible. Gaucho looked toward the trunk where Betty was held and took three breaths before Aidan fired every round in his clip. The bullets ripped massive holes through Gaucho's chest. He screamed in excruciating pain until a final bullet tore into his throat and silenced him.

Sebastian watched the massacre unfold but the loss of Ms. Jordan still paralyzed him. He wanted to run away, but tossing her to the side like road kill was something he could not muster up the strength to do. Sebastian was also tired of running. Escaping that day only meant there would be more days he had to look over his shoulders. The Capilini family wasn't going to stop chasing him. He wanted to survive the day, but the dead woman in his lap reminded him how costly it had become for others to extend their hand to help him. Aidan was only steps away when Sebastian closed his eyes and waited for his life to be taken. He heard the sound of rapid gunfire, but the pain he expected never came. When he opened his eyes he saw his would-be killer lying in front of him dead. His saving grace was the one person it had always been. Harrison had taken a bullet in the shoulder. He played dead until the right opportunity presented itself. Gaucho's death happened so quickly he didn't have time to act. But, from his position on the ground, he was able to fire all sixteen shells in his Glock nine-millimeter, hitting Aidan in the eye first then his torso.

At the end of the shootout, four people were on the ground dead. Sebastian continued rocking back and forth as he held Ms. Jordan. Harrison survived being shot, but he was weak from losing a lot of blood and needed help. He used the last bit of strength he had to walk over to Sebastian.

"Hey, kid, we gotta go. This place is gonna be crawlin' with cops and if we wanna keep you under the radar and alive we gotta go now," Harrison said.

Sebastian didn't utter a word. His eyes were locked on the beautiful face of the woman he felt he had a chance to fall in love with.

"Snap out of it, kid! She's gone, and we gotta go!"

He pulled at Sebastian's clothes a few times before he finally heard a rebuttal.

"Fuck you!!!!!" Sebastian yelled.

Both stared at each other for a minute straight. Their silence was broken by Betty's cries for help.

"Get me outta here. Clarence! Help me!" she screamed.

She was unaware the man she called for was dead just two feet away from the trunk she was trapped in.

"Fuck it. You're on your own," Harrison said.

He had enough of Sebastian not listening to him and

he wasn't going to get shot again trying to be his savior. Harrison's bullet wound only appeared to be a flesh wound, but his misdiagnosis and rapid loss of blood put him in a bind he could not get out of. He walked as fast as he could to his car, but dizziness began to set in. His brisk steps became stumbles until he collapsed on the ground. Staring toward the sky he fought hard to keep his eyes open. Hearing approaching police sirens erased his last remaining will to escape. Harrison let his eyes close.

JAMAL A. BENJAMIN

Chapter 26

The beeping sound of his heart monitor was the first sign indicating Harrison's survival. He heard the machine when he woke up inside his hospital room. He was too weak to sit up, but he was able to move his head in a position where he could get a full observation of his whereabouts. The room was empty, but he could see a police officer stationed outside his room. He wasn't handcuffed to the bed so he knew he hadn't been arrested. His memory of how he got to the hospital was non-existent. He did remember the events that led to him nursing wounds in the hospital. His recollection of the shootout made him wonder where Sebastian had gone. He wondered how far he'd gotten or if he was still alive. Both questions were answered soon after they entered his head. He could hear hard bottom shoes walking in the hallway toward his room. The footsteps grew louder by the second. When the echoing footsteps ceased, Harrison heard voices outside his door. He could tell one was female and the other was male. Both individuals entered dressed in business suit attire. They were federal agents. Agent Stevenson introduced herself as the lead investigator. The tall, long-haired brunette would be pleasing to any heterosexual male's eyes, but Harrison soon found out she was a pit bull dressed in a grey pants suit.

"It's not my birthday and it's not Christmas, but when I got the call about what was going on here, it made me feel kinda like that grade school girl who got everything she ever wanted," said Agent Stevenson.

"I don't know what you're getting at or talking about," Harrison said.

"Testing my intelligence is not in you or your son's best interest." She knew that threat would immediately grab Harrison's attention. Over the next few minutes, all the details of her federal investigation and everything else Harrison needed to know was laid out for him. The FBI was taking over the investigation into the murders of Stanley Gaucho Morrison and Sophia Jordan, as well as the attempted murder of Barkley Capleton. The mention of those names was a clear indication of what the FBI knew, and they knew enough to make life difficult for Harrison for a very long time.

"What do you want?" Harrison asked.

Agent Robertson put his hand on his partner's shoulder to let her know he could handle that question. He was also someone who didn't mince his words, nor sugar coat them. He told Harrison that the bureau wanted to bring the Capilini family down and he was finally going to use the knowledge he acquired as a dirty cop for law enforcement.

"You're either gonna play nice or get fucked, and this is not a gang bang you want any parts of. You wanna roll the dice, you get charged with a boatload of crimes that you won't beat and we'll brand you a snitch. Which means you and your family will likely be dead before the end of the year," Agent Robertson said.

Backed into a corner he could not slither out of, Harrison knew he had to make a deal. Before he signed off on playing ball with the feds, he made one request. He wanted to see Barkley one last time. The request was denied. The rejection did not come from the federal agents. They were just the messengers. Barkley made it clear he would only reveal everything he knew if they kept Harrison away from him. Harrison did receive some closure. He was handed a two-page letter written from Barkley, which read like an obituary. He praised Harrison for being his saving grace several times. Every single heroic feat was not mentioned, but it clearly stated he was thankful for his role in keeping him alive. The next few paragraphs focused on taking responsibility. He did not pull the trigger but Barkley felt responsible for Ms. Jordan's death.

Barkley stayed clear of hopping on a soapbox to preach righteousness in his letter. He focused on how the entire ordeal changed him. His final message to Harrison closed with graciousness. It read:

I now know what it means to be a man. I owe a lot of that to you. It's time for me to stop dreaming. This experience has awakened me in many ways. More importantly, it has given me scars that will never truly heal, and I like that. The pain will always be there, and will serve as a reminder of how my actions will always affect the ones I cherish the most.

Goodbye.

Harrison stared at the letter holding back tears. He held all of them off but one. It trickled down his face until he wiped it away. It was closure.

He hadn't been called Barkley much since he arrived in Sandusky. No one knew who he really was. After getting his walking papers from the feds, Barkley was ready to start fresh. He looked forward to new beginnings, but also walked out of the hospital wrapped in emotional turmoil. His longtime friend was about to disappear from his life completely and the woman he barely knew, but felt so much for, was dead. He felt her blood was on his hands. Barkley's mind could only generate memories of the brief moments he shared with Ms. Jordan as he walked slowly away from the hospital. A wave of opportunity was still coming to Sandusky for Barkley. Any words about who he was or his involvement in the violent death of a beloved local had not surfaced yet. He knew this was the case when Coach Hankerson pulled up beside him in his Ford pick-up. He had already learned of his cousin's death. There was a look of relief on his face when he saw Barkley. That was a clear indication that he didn't know the whole story.

"You don't how happy I am to see you alive. No one's answering the family's questions and all we know is that we lost a hell of a woman. Where were you walking off to?" Coach Hankerson said.

Barkley thought to come clean right then and there, but he didn't want the coach to hit the accelerator and run him over. He knew once Coach Hankerson found out the connection he had to his cousin's death, their relationships was bound to change. He couldn't come up with a destination in his head, so Barkley just shrugged his shoulders in response to the question. The coach ordered him to get in the truck. They took several long winding back roads on the way to Coach Hankerson's home. During the ride, Barkley tried to formulate a story that sounded less damaging than the truth. He couldn't. He felt he owed Coach Hankerson an honest answer to whatever he asked. He just didn't know how to tell him or what words to use.

When they arrived, Barkley could only think of jumping out of the car and running until he couldn't run anymore. With no motivation to run for the hills, coupled with an invitation to join coach Hankerson inside his home, the idea of escaping from the difficult encounter heading his way quickly faded. When they entered, the house was empty. Both were circling the truth when they took seats in the living room. Coach Hankerson was trying to figure out what questions to ask to get to the details behind his cousin's death, while Barkley was trying to figure how he was going to reveal the truth. He decided he was going to be the first to speak and let the chips fall where they may.

"Coach, I know you got a lot of questions. I'm not sure if I have the answers to all of them. But what I'm about to say is gonna make things a little clearer," Barkley said in a humbled voice.

Barkley decided to bare his soul to Coach Hankerson, starting with his childhood. Barkley could tell Coach Hankerson was getting antsy with his roundabout way of telling him the reason why his cousin was dead.

"I know this seems like I'm stalling but I'm not. This will all be tied together soon." Barkley said. Coach Hankerson allowed Barkley to continue his story, but his frustration was simmering and ready to erupt. Barkley sped up his storytelling and began to describe how he met Kevlar. "After leaving school I hooked up with this guy named Kevlar. He was putting together a street ball team, and wanted me to be a part of it. This was my one shot out of a life that was headed nowhere fast. I had to do it," Barkley said. He continued his story, describing to Coach Hankerson the lavish ghetto-fabulous life he had thrust upon him.

"Money just seemed to be falling in my lap once I got down with Kevlar and the team. And there were women. Oh, the women were like those video chicks. I even had a threesome, and that was awesome. Before that…"

"Enough! What the fuck happened to my cousin. You're here talking about champagne, women, and all types of shit that I really don't give a fuck about. Why is my cousin dead?" Coach Hankerson yelled.

"She's dead because of me."

Barkley's words were like a shotgun blast to the face for Coach Hankerson. He didn't know how to react. His body sunk into the couch, with his eyes locked on the hardwood floor. Silence engulfed the entire house. Barkley knew now was the best time to make an exit, but he couldn't. He had nowhere else to go. He had no family. He had nothing. His only chance for a semblance of a life hung on the shoulders of Coach Hankerson. He'd already revealed his role in Ms. Jordan's death, now it was time to go forward with the details. His voice trembled as he spoke of the chain of events leading to the prior day's violent climax. Barkley tried, but he couldn't utter the words to describe Ms. Jordan's last moments alive. He could only say what he thought might soothe the pain coach Hankerson was experiencing.

"I held her until she wasn't there anymore," Barkley said.

"I'm gonna need you to get the fuck out of my house," Coach Hankerson said. He repeated the instruction, but in an angrier voice. He was through with Barkley. His attempt to do right by him only lead to bloodshed at his doorstep, and he wasn't gonna put anymore family at risk.

211

When he saw his words weren't motivation enough for Barkley to exit, he took more of a physical approach. The portly middle-aged coach didn't have much of a chance to carry Barkley out but he tried with every ounce of strength. The pair tussled and fell to the ground. Barkley was absorbing blows but was not fighting back. He was just trying to hold on long enough for Coach Hankerson to tire himself out. He grabbed onto the staircase banister and held tight. After twenty seconds, Coach Hankerson's machine gun-style attack took its toll on him. His exertion of rage and emotion sapped most of his energy. He was able to muster a few words in between taking deep breaths. He tried to fight back tears as he spoke.

"My baby... cousin... is dead. She's dead!" he said.

Slowly, Coach Hankerson picked himself up from the floor. When he finally made it to his feet, he hovered over Barkley for a few seconds. Barkley broke the silence with another plea for help.

"Coach, I can't begin to understand how you feel, but I'm begging you. Please don't turn your back on me. The one thing I learned about your cousin was she had a big heart. She wanted to help people in need. I wanna do that," Barkley said as he began rising to his feet.

Both men were tired from their brief scuffle on the floor, but that did nothing to lessen or cease the tension between them. Barkley felt once he stopped talking he was dead in the water. He knew he hadn't said anything to make Coach Hankerson take him in. He wanted to keep talking but couldn't come up with any more words. At the conclusion of his pleas and apologies, Coach Hankerson turned his back and walked toward the front door. Barkley knew once the coach opened the door, his second chance at a meaningful life was gone. He tried to come up with more words but couldn't. With his head lowered Barkley walked toward the door hoping to receive sign of good things to come. Only two steps separated Barkley from his coach, when it seemed like a change of heart was occurring. Coach Hankerson paused with his hand on the doorknob. His pause was driven by the memories he created with Barkley over the short amount of time they knew each other. In a brief period of time he recognized the special athletic gifts Barkley possessed, and in that same time span he also grew an attachment to him.

Coach Hankerson was conflicted about throwing him out. After all, tossing him into the unknown would be dishonoring Ms. Jordan's memory. Still, the pain was too great for him to look past Barkley's involvement in his beloved cousin's violent death. He opened the door.

"Get the fuck out and good luck kid."

Barkley's entire body felt empty as he was being thrown to the wolves of the world once again. In his mind, he'd accepted Coach Hankerson's decision, but he couldn't move. Both stood frozen in the same position unable to close that chapter in their lives. Neither could utter a word. The silence was broken by a phone call in the nearby kitchen. Coach Hankerson just stared at the door, waiting for Barkley to make his exit. After seven rings, the answering machine picked up.

Hello, you've reached the home of the Hankersons. Please leave a clear and concise message, so we can return your call at our earliest convenience. BEEP!

"Hi, this is Rick Pitino, head coach of the men's college basketball team at Louisville. I'm very interested in setting up a campus visit for Sebastian. We'd love for him to see what receiving a full scholarship and becoming a Cardinal at Louisville can do for his career. Please give me a call back on my cell phone number, 502-555-7897."

It was great news, but under the current circumstances, it was like Barkley owned a lottery ticket he had no way of cashing. His head stayed lowered through the entire message. Coach Hankerson continued staring out the doorway. The phone rang again. A second coach left a message.

"This is Thad Matta from Ohio State University…"

A third call.

"Hi, this is Jim Boeheim calling from Syracuse University…"

A fourth call.

"Hello, this John Calipari, head coach for the Kentucky Wildcats…"

By the end of the fourth call, Barkley's head was still lowered. He raised it slowly when he heard the front door close.

When he returned his head to its normal position, he discovered Coach Hankerson staring at him on the verge of shedding tears.

"I really wanna let you rot in hell for the death of my cousin, but that wouldn't be what she'd wanted me to do. She'd want me to help…to take care of you. And that's what I'm gonna do. This is about her and only her. For the rest of your fucking life, I want you to remember the life that was sacrificed so you can live. Remember her in everything you fucking do, because if you don't, I'm gonna be there to kick your ass until you do. You understand that?" Coach Hankerson asked.

Still shocked and speechless from what just

occurred, Barkley nodded his head in the affirmative.

Coach Hankerson walked toward Barkley and pulled out his phone.

"We've got some phone calls to make."

THE END

About the Author

Jamal Benjamin grew up in Queens, New York. He currently resides in Staten Island and has worked in the television news industry for 15 years. As a producer with CBS News and NBC News, he has worked on national news stories such as the 2008 Texas Polygamist compound raid and covered the Democrat and Republican conventions during 2012 Presidential election. Jamal's work has been featured on the CBS Evening News, MSNBC and has earned an Emmy nomination for his work with the CBS Early Show. For more information about Jamal visit www.facebook.com/BenGeeBucks or Twitter: @JamalABenjamin.

www.ingramcontent.com/pod-product-compliance
Lightning Source LLC
Chambersburg PA
CBHW051502170626
46811CB00002B/594